YOUR PLACE IS HERE NOW

JASON FISCHER

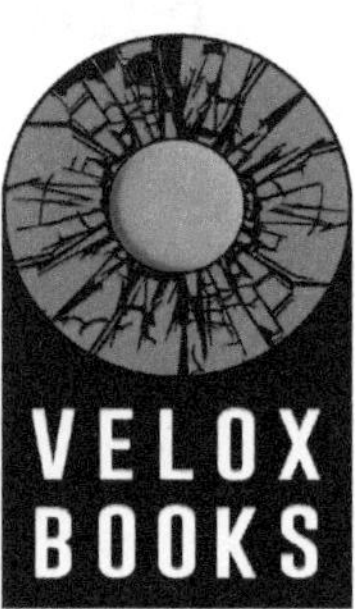

Published by arrangement with the author.

Copyright © 2025 by Jason Fischer.

All rights reserved.

YOU'RE READING ANOTHER TERRIFYING COLLECTION FROM

**FOLLOW VELOX TO KEEP
THE NIGHTMARES COMING:**

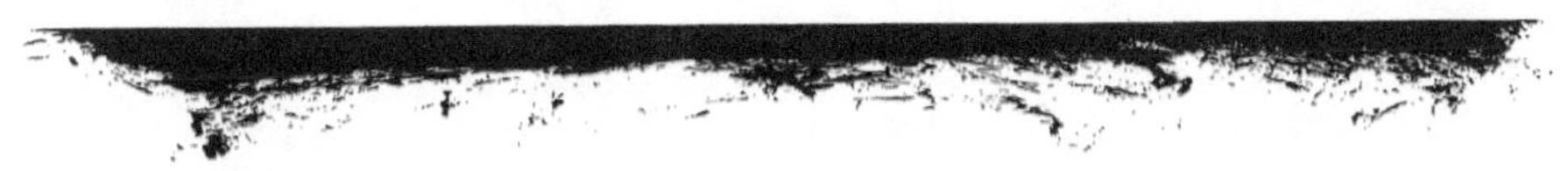

CONTENTS

INVOLUNTARY DEPENDENT

They watched the preteen pull the cloth sack over his head. It was wrinkled, dirty, and had a jagged streak of lipstick where the mouth should've been. There were two tiny holes for the nose and shiny black buttons sewn for eyes just below the synthetic curly hair. Under the plastic buttons were small, uneven holes that Joshua could see through.

Melissa stared in disbelief at their unexpected houseguest and then at her partner. Kim looked at her pleadingly in response, begging for silence. It was the look reserved for polite conversation at a dinner party, not to conceal her disdain over her brother's actions.

His eyes were filled with hate as he disrobed the doll that he held over his knee, the doll he had referred to as his *punishment self.* With practiced strokes, he relentlessly beat the backside of the doll, each strike resulting in a resounding *thump* that filled the tiny spare room of the condo. Both women cringed as if the blows had landed on them rather than the lifeless toy.

Muffled words came through the sack. "I told you! I told you, be good, or you will get your punishment, stupid." His words sounded like they had come from another room, like a ventriloquist's trick.

In a voice that was so calm it scared Melissa, Kim said, "Okay, Joshua. That's enough now."

He looked up and cocked his head far enough back to see through the tiny space the stretched material would allow. "It ain't, neither, and don't call me that name. Not when I'm like this." He flipped his head back in an exaggerated gesture, causing the wig to bounce back playfully.

"Please do as I say. That's enough." Her voice rose, yet she didn't sound as if she were scolding him. The words were more like polite requests than demands.

Reluctantly, he pulled the mask from his head, causing his unwashed hair to hang across his red, blotchy face. He carefully folded the mask and put it next to him on the futon that would be his bed for the foreseeable future. Then, with delicate care, he lifted the doll's pants, covering its exposed behind. When the clothing was back in place, he lifted the smiling toy and hugged it, leaving its limbs to dangle freely as he softly hummed a nursery rhyme to it.

Melissa's heart was racing as she stared at the black and white doll. It was nearly three feet tall and looked like a leftover prize from a carnival. The painted canvas material was matted in spots, as if it were filled with tufts of worn cotton.

"Thank you, Joshua," Kim whispered.

He ignored her, turning slightly away from the two women. He hugged his doll tighter in his arms, squeezing his eyes shut and humming louder.

"I'm going to go to the other room for a few minutes and talk about some adult things with Mel. I'll be right back."

"You know you aren't supposed to lay with a woman like you've been, don't ya?" Joshua let his doll drop and turned back, staring. Glaring at Melissa, he pulled at a strand of his oily hair, twirling it between his thumb and forefinger. With his free hand, he caressed the mask, making small circles on top of the fabric and tracing the outline of the obscene lips.

"Joshua, don't be rude. You sit quietly, and I'll be right back," Kim said and nodded toward the door.

They exited the small room and headed to the kitchen. Melissa said as quietly as her nerves would allow, "What the fuck was that?"

"I know that was disturbing, and I'm sorry I didn't warn you." Kim looked at the shared wall between the kitchen and the bedroom. Lifting one finger to her lips for quiet, she spoke to the puck-like device on the table. "Play my relaxing playlist." In the background, *Moonlight Sonata* filled the room, adding to the somber mood of the cramped space.

"Disturbing? That was terrifying. What happened to that kid? Why's he doing that, and why're you so, so... calm?"

"It's the way he..." Kim paused, closing her eyes and squeezing her fists. "... the way *we* were raised."

"What does that mean?" Melissa moved toward her, her arms open.

Kim quickly raised her hands and said, "Please don't. Not right now. If I start crying, I might not stop."

Melissa took a step back, awkwardly wrapping her arms around herself. In their four years together, she could never remember having been rejected quite like that. As she fought to think of her partner's feeling over her own, the music echoed in the small space, seeming to be in sync with her mood.

"I told you before that I had a nontraditional upbringing. My mother had... well, very odd ways to teach us to deal with our emotions. Believe me, I know how freaked out you must be right now." Her eyes glazed over with tears as she sniffled deeply, somehow stopping them from streaming out. "I know I would be if I were you, but you have to understand that my mother was just trying to teach us to cope."

"By beating a creepy-ass doll?" Melissa's eyes flashed as she waved her hand toward her lover.

"It is just a role-playing device. She would have us wear a mother or father mask and then administer punishment to our doll, which represented our negative behaviors." She looked down, suddenly shy. "After we got the anger out, she would talk to us and teach us how to react more positively."

Melissa had no siblings, aunts, or uncles, only a mother who had passed away while she was young, so she was struggling to understand how such insane behavior could be forgiven.

Spending a good portion of your formative years in foster care greatly skewed one's perspectives on what to expect from others. "I'm sorry. I know you've been through a lot, but I have to say it. If you're defending what we just witnessed, I'm speechless, hon."

"I'm not defending anything!" Kim's hands went to the sides of her head, disappearing into her thick, curly hair. "Too much has happened in the last twenty-four hours. I don't even know what I'm thinking anymore. I'm ashamed, scared, and don't know what to say to you right now, but even if he is acting strange, that's still my little brother. He just buried his mother, and now he's seeing me for the first time in over four years and is trying to cope with all of it."

As she trembled all over, her tears finally came in streams. She fought to breathe between gasps of air. Melissa moved to her and gently stroked the back of her head. Kim willingly embraced her and convulsed with sobs. Melissa began questioning the decision to let the boy stay with them.

Despite her own apprehension, as Kim quieted down, Melissa whispered, "It's going to be okay. Whatever we have to do, we're going to do because we are strong enough to get through this." Melissa now wished she had insisted that Kim attend the funeral when the call came last week. It was apparent that she needed closure from the life she had left behind. She knew Kim had had a very complicated relationship with her mother. It was understandable being raised in such an isolated, rural area without a father and with a much younger brother to commiserate with, yet she had never guessed it was so dark. None of the talks they had had regarding her upbringing had ever hinted at the depravity Melissa had just witnessed in the other room.

Wishing she could take all the pain away, she hugged Kim tighter, so tightly she barely heard her squeak out, "I'm sorry..."

"There's nothing to be sorry for." Melissa said, caressing the back of Kim's head and patting down her curls. With her eyes closed, she tried to pretend none of this was happening, that they were just having an ordinary day filled with the peace they had worked so hard to carve out from their place.

Kim's warm breath on her chest encouraged her to lie. "Everything's going to be all right." Melissa sincerely wished she could believe her own words, but she knew nothing would ever be remotely the same. She had lived through transitions like this before and knew better than to fool herself. This much change couldn't come without consequences. Hiding the apprehension in her voice, she said, "What can I do?"

"I wish I knew." Even with the loud background music, rhythmic grunting echoed through the wall. Glancing up, she said, "Do you hear that?"

"Yes." They headed back to the room where they had left Joshua. When they opened the door, he was wearing his father mask and was spanking a girl doll. Its hair color and style were identical to Kim's.

"Joshua, you stop that this instant!"

"I ain't Joshua no more." He kept at the beating. Each strike ended in a dull *thump* against the worn fabric.

"If you don't take off that mask right now, I will kick you out!"

"No, you won't, neither." In defiance, he stared through the eyeholes in the mask and whipped his doll faster. Each brutal stroke was louder than the last.

Kim moved quickly to the bed and ripped the doll from his lap. She held it dangling between her thumb and forefinger as if it were acidic, examining its distorted handmade features from as far away as her arm would allow. Finally, she tossed it into the hallway, the unsightly fabric twirling in the air. Before she could grab hold of the mask, Joshua quickly removed it and hid it up his shirt. He leaned forward protectively, giving him the appearance of being pregnant. In his thick southern accent, he said, "I'm trying to help you, Sister. You need to be cleansed of your wrongdoings."

"Joshua, I'll not have this behavior in my house."

He rubbed the mask through his shirt. "But we gotta fix this, Kimmy. Real quick, too. Before she, well, you know."

"Joshua, you'll be staying here for some time until we figure out what's best. You need to understand that things're different here, and it's not like it was back home."

"I wish I was still at home with Ma."

"I know, but that isn't possible." She sat down next to her younger sibling. Tentatively, he put his hand over hers, and they sat wordlessly, looking into his open knapsack and staring at the other doll's tattered appendages hanging out over the top.

"You know that ain't true. She's still wit' us." The young boy's voice quivered as he spoke. "She always will be, like the book promised."

Kim nodded in quiet agreement. "Everything will be right... in time."

Melissa stood, trying not to stare at the mask peeping out from under the boy's shirt. For the first time in their four-year relationship, she stared at her partner and saw a stranger.

Repulsed, her mind filled with all the relationships she had endured before meeting the woman she knew she was meant to be with. Nothing had come between them before, not even their ten- year age gap. But this felt different. As she walked out of the room, she heard them humming a hymn she had recognized from her childhood days in the choir. The sound did little to quiet her already frantic mind.

The next morning, after showering, Melissa opened the door to the spare room. Lying next to Joshua, Kim looked much younger than her twenty-four years. The light from the hallway woke her. She extracted herself from the futon, and they walked to the kitchen.

Melissa slid a mug with the inscription *Have a great day!* beneath a smiley face that hovered over Niagara Falls across the table. The ridiculously cheap cup was a joke souvenir from their first vacation together. They had driven in Melissa's beat-up car from New Bremen, Illinois, to New York a few weeks after they started dating. Looking at the rushing water was when they knew their relationship was going somewhere. The memory usually brought a nostalgic warmth, but the tension of the last few hours took even that little bit of happiness away. "How did you sleep?"

"Good, I guess. I don't remember much after I closed my eyes." She grabbed her matted hair and pulled it back over her shoulders. "I assume Joshua slept through the night. At least I don't remember him moving at all."

"He was up to use the bathroom."

"Did he wake you?"

"Not purposefully. He's as quiet as you are when he wanders around in the dark." She smirked, hoping to see Kim smile.

Wide-eyed, she asked, "Are you angry with me?"

"Why would you ask that?" Melissa reached across the small table that barely fit into the cramped room and grabbed her girlfriend's hand.

"I feel bad."

"Why?"

"For what you seen yesterday."

"Don't think about that." Melissa shook her head quickly, as if it would help erase the words.

"I know, but you shouldn't have to deal with that."

"I don't feel like I have to do anything. This is just something *we* are going through right now." There was a quick glimpse of hope in Kim's stare. Like a switch being flipped, it instantly went away.

"Mel, I don't know what to do next. I can't believe I agreed to bring ..." Kim glanced toward the hallway with a guilty look. "... him here. I don't know what I was thinking."

"You were being a good sister and a responsible person. There is nothing wrong with that." Melissa usually kept her past buried—hiding from hurtful things was a binding force in their relationship—but now she chose to say, "Believe me, when your only connection to the adult world leaves you, it's very important to have someone look out for you."

"I understand that, but what are we going to do? We can't raise him."

The eager look for support reminded Melissa of first meeting Kim when she came to town. She arrived with little more than the clothes on her back. Thinking of a woman teaching life skills with hideous masks, she could understand Kim's taking the risk of starting a life with nothing and her reluctance to ever speak of her upbringing. "We have time to think about what's best for all of us. Right now, let's just focus on the next few days."

"I guess." Kim absently twirled a strand of her blonde hair, the gesture mirroring her brother's movements yesterday. "You know, my ma wasn't completely insane."

"I never said she was."

"All that stuff with the mask really was her way of helping. She was raised in a community that was... well, different." The strands of hair made it into her mouth. "Everything she did was with good intentions, and it ain't like she didn't care." After a long silence, she added, "It ain't possible to explain, but she's just different from others."

Melissa felt uneasy as she heard the accent that Kim had fought so hard to hide come back. It was as if she was willingly regressing into someone else. Melissa felt an impulse to shake it out of her mouth, feeling like it would bring back the woman she loved and pull her from a path that was going to lead to sadness.

The rawness of the emotion brought an unexpected bitterness. "I'm not judging you here, but you do know that if he is going to stay, he will have to give up those dolls. They just aren't healthy." She didn't bother hiding her disgust.

"I will talk to him about them."

She didn't really want to know, but the words came out anyway. "When you were little, you used to... punish them as well?"

"Yes." She grabbed Melissa's hands with both of her own, squeezing them for emphasis. "Really, it isn't always as weird as it seemed yesterday. Ma used to read psychology books that she collected from library sales; most were very outdated but had some decent information. Like I said, she had odd ways, but her intentions were always good."

"Were her intentions good when she taught him to be homophobic?" She immediately knew the answer when Kim looked down shamefully.

"No! She wasn't perfect, Mel."

The resentment she was bottling up became uncorked. "Did you sleep in there last night because you were ashamed to be with me when he is here?"

She finally looked up, biting her lower lip so hard it was turning white. "No, not at all. I was just exhausted and fell asleep there."

She desperately wanted to believe her, but it was difficult. "You know you can't hide who you are." Melissa's stomach turned as her own youthful struggles, which she had fought so far to repress, bubbled up. She knew better than to antagonize Kim, but couldn't stop herself. All the stress was taking over. She folded her arms across her chest, staring deeply into Kim's eyes, urging compassion to stop the fight before it took off.

"You don't have to say that to me. I know who I am."

"We will see, won't we?" The words were spoken so quietly that it was as if her lips were trying to protect her from saying something that couldn't be taken back. Before Kim had a chance to respond with more justifications, Joshua entered the room wearing the mother mask now. It was a collage of blue eyeshadow, red lips, and blush. The only human feature was his dull eyes poking through the narrow slits. Not containing her anger, Melissa said, "Take that off now!" She barely kept herself from adding, *"You little freak."*

Joshua continued staring, scratching at his chest in perfect circles as his eyes moved from left to right. Kim got up and put her arm around him. She whispered something, and he slowly removed the mask. As it cleared his face, he gave Melissa a smile. His lips curled back, exposing his crooked teeth.

Having had enough of the shocking display, she wordlessly left the room. The tension from the last few hours was making it hard to think straight.

As she closed the door to their bedroom, she heard the two of them giggling, each noise going through her. Every second that ticked by, Melissa felt like an out-of-control infection was making its way into her partner, permanently changing her. Walking to the bathroom full of rage, she noticed her hairbrush lying on the counter in front of the sink. It was not where she had left it.

As she examined the bristles, she realized that they were picked clean of any loose strands of hair. Instinctively, she looked at the wastebasket. It was empty, except for a few tissues at the bottom. Remembering the maxi pad she had placed there before her morning shower, she immediately thought Joshua had snuck in and was rummaging around the small bathroom. Suddenly, nothing seemed real anymore.

It now felt like time had a different quality, altering her perception and sense of well-being. Every vein felt like it was beating to an intense rhythm, heating her skin. She clenched her fists and fought to focus her racing mind, attempting to find logic. Knowing she was too angry to be rational, she fought the instinct to accuse him of raiding through her waste. She was either confused or he was baiting her into a fight she wouldn't win. As she struggled to continue her morning routine, Melissa ignored the sense that her life was going in a direction she had no way of controlling.

Over the next few days, the siblings grew closer, and Melissa spent most of her time alone in her bedroom like a passenger on a vessel she didn't want to be on. Kim entered their former room only now for changes of clothes. She spent her nights sleeping next to her brother.

The dolls continuously found their way into different parts of the condo. Melissa was currently staring at the boy doll sitting on the kitchen chair they had found in a secondhand shop. The dining room furniture was the first thing they had bought when they got the condo.

Seeing the abomination in the place she felt safest in the world was unsettling, straining her already taut nerves. They spent most of their time in this room; it was windowless and much too small, but it made them feel insulated from the city and all its energy. Remembering all the mornings they had spent there together drinking coffee and talking endlessly, having the doll there was more than she could handle. Her plan of giving her partner space and time to work everything out now seemed foolish—maybe even dangerous. Melissa called out, "Kim!" After half a minute, her girlfriend entered the kitchen.

"Yeah?"

Seeing Kim dressed only in a wrinkled T-shirt and her hair disheveled brought memories of hundreds of tender moments echoing in Melissa's mind. Longing to hug Kim tight and forget all that had happened, she eventually said, "I thought we talked about these dolls."

"We did. I'm sorry that he left it out." She reached over and picked up the boy doll. The palms of both of her hands were an intense red.

Thinking of Kim possibly administering punishment to the dolls, Melissa's eye twitched.

Knowing any contact would weaken her resolve, she said, "I thought you were going to take them from him."

"I will, Mel. I just feel like I have to do it the right way."

"What does that mean?" Melissa looked her up and down. Not only was her accent stronger than ever, something else was different, but she couldn't easily distinguish what.

"I don't want to do it too quickly."

"Why not?"

"I was reading about it in a book."

"You found a book that talks about handling punishment dolls?" With a bewildered look, Melissa tilted her head back, trying not to chastise her any further.

"Yes. Josh brought it from Ma's house."

The accent grew thicker with each syllable. Tension settled in Melissa's temples as her desperation built. It took effort to keep sarcasm out of her tone. "And you think it's a good idea to follow what it says?"

Playfully, Kim shrugged like a shy schoolgirl, twisting her hips from left to right, both innocent and alluring at the same time. "Not sure what else I can do."

Watching Kim act so vulnerable slowed her anger and caused confusion. The sense that they were growing further apart as every second ticked past was more than she could handle.

Exasperated, Melissa moved tentatively to Kim, reaching for her. Kim's look quickly turned to one of repulsion as she turned, pushing Melissa's hand away.

Melissa grunted. "Really?" she said as her face warmed. "I just don't feel in the mood right now."

"Well, when might ya?" She felt ashamed the second the mock words left her mouth. "You shouldn't make fun of people 'cause the way they talk." Her chin was buried into her neck as she gave a sly stare. "It's ain't polite."

"What's happening to you?" she bit off. *"Why are you becoming a hillbilly?"* The thought felt tangible, weighing her down as she realized how insensitive she was becoming.

"Nothin.'"

"How can you say that? You're turning back into the person you came to this city to escape. That's not who you want to be anymore." She wanted to say, *"Right?"* but let it go, knowing the answer was far too dangerous. Her voice cracked as she added, "And you don't even want to touch me."

"There will be time for that. Right now, I'm still grieving."

It was the first time Kim had sounded remotely like herself. Believing the lie because she needed it to cling to, Melissa said, "Hon, you promise that's all?"

"Of course. Things will get normal soon enough. We just need time to adjust to all of this." She hugged the doll to her chest with an absent-minded expression on her face. The worn fabric face was turned away from her, its monstrous, fixed smile glaring at Melissa. "Sorry, but I gotta get back to Joshua now. I'm helping him with his math equations. He's missed far too much learnin' over the last few weeks. We can talk later after he gets to sleep, okay?" She gently caressed the back of Melissa's hand with her fingertips.

"Okay." As she watched her head down the dark hallway, the sense that she was losing Kim was strong enough to bring tears.

An hour later, a large crate arrived by courier. Before Melissa could open it, Kim and her brother pulled what was shaped like a cheap coffin into their room, explaining that it was more of their mother's belongings.

Later that night, Melissa heard what she believed was a sewing machine and an unfamiliar female voice coming from their room. She sporadically tapped on their door, and they would not answer. Melissa knew she could force her way into the room, but she was not up to any more confrontations. She went to bed, where she stared off into the darkness, listening to various whispers and the whir of the machine through the thin walls.

In the brief moments when the machine's noise stopped, all she could hear was rhythmic slaps. Staring in the direction of the room, she tried her best to will sense into Kim and bring her back to the woman she was desperately in love with. Melissa knew that an ultimatum was warranted, but her insecurity at being with a woman years younger than her stopped her.

Thinking of all the loneliness and isolation that she had gone through before Kim, she wished she had the strength to leave temporarily, if only to emphasize her point. As she slipped off to a restless sleep, she began questioning her own sanity.

Later that evening, Melissa awoke to someone massaging her back. Her mind prompted her to see a doll lying in the bed next to her. Relief spread when her eyes focused enough to recognize Kim. She wanted to say a hundred things but didn't want to spoil their first real moment alone together in so long.

Kim caressed her shoulders lovingly, the light trace of her fingers sending chills down Melissa's spine. Slowly, Kim worked her way down to Melissa's breasts, instantly relieving all of Melissa's pent-up frustration with her touch. Their eager lips eventually found each other in the dark, probing each other wildly with passion.

After a moment, Kim paused, brushing her tongue along Melissa's neck, and whispered, "Spank me."

"What?" The thought equally repulsed Melissa and turned her on.

Kim pulled off her jeans, revealing silk panties. She lay across Melissa's lap, writhing up and down. "Do it... hard."

Melissa, not fully understanding why, obeyed. The first slap was playful. Kim writhed, arching her back. Massaging her taut flesh, Melissa struck again with a little more force. Hearing her partner whine in pleasure, she slapped harder.

Each subsequent strike grew louder, followed by a deep, satisfied moan. After a minute, her hand ached, but she didn't stop. She kept striking the same spot, relishing each time her fingertips came into contact with her partner's bare skin. Both panted as the rhythm increased, creating a symphony of moans. After each strike, Kim thrust upward every time Melissa's hand came free, as if she couldn't stand being away from Melissa's touch. The anticipation of the shared pain and pleasure brought a delicious dizziness.

Lost in the moment, she heard Kim's muffled voice call, "More. Harder."

Feeling more turned on than she ever had, Melissa, in her peripheral vision, saw the shiny buttons of the mother mask through the darkness. The painted lips of the fabric stretched as Kim called out, "Don't stop now!"

Melissa, without thought, used both hands to push Kim off her lap in swift motion. Looking at her lover wearing lingerie and the dirty mask made her want to vomit. "A mask?"

"You're really sick, aren't you?" The expressionless face glared back. Melissa slid back, getting caught up in the sheets and feeling immediate claustrophobic angst as she struggled to free her now frozen limbs. "Get out. Now!"

"Please don't be like that. I need you." Kim stood up, pulling the mask from her head. Her hair was matted to her forehead and held there through her perspiration. She hid the mask behind her back as she leaned forward, trying for a kiss.

Melissa, struggling to free her arms, shook her head. "Not like this. No." She inched backward on the mattress. The sense of violation made her feel sick, as she squirmed the few inches the tangled fabric would allow. "I won't do this anymore." Tears streamed out, sensing that the love they had shared was now lost forever, overtaken with disgust.

"Don't you want me anymore?" Kim asked, leaning strategically forward and emphasizing the curves of her body.

Mel's torso was shaking as she clutched the sheet, fighting for freedom. "Just leave, Kim! Please, just leave."

With a snort, Kim put her hand on her hip, thrusting as if she were posing for a dirty magazine. In a sultry voice, she leaned over, putting her mouth close to Melissa's ear, and said, "I know you want it as much as I do." She kissed her earlobe, slipping her hand between her girlfriend's legs before adding, "Just let go and take what you want."

A jolt of energy surged through Melissa. No longer able to control the urge that was consuming every inch of her being, she pulled Kim onto the bed. With her arms wrapped around her, the coarse material of the mask brushed her fingertips, making her cringe. Ignoring all instincts except for one, she took Kim, giving in to a passion that she knew she couldn't survive without.

The following day, a drenching rain beat against the window, hiding the sun. Melissa wore a baggy sweater and sweatpants, wanting to hide her sexuality and the shame it had brought after the previous night. Before leaving her bedroom, she placed her ear against the door and slowly opened it to ensure safe passage. The spare room stood open.

Wanting to leave, but knowing she couldn't abandon the only person who truly mattered behind without trying one more time, she walked to the open doorway. Lying on the bed, their involuntary dependent was asleep. Next to him was the life-sized doll. It lay with its arm around him, with the mother mask on, staring upward toward the ceiling. The sewing machine was in the center of the room, surrounded by hundreds of neatly folded, tiny clothes.

The sound of dishes clanging wiped away the thoughts of satanic rituals and possession.

Closing the door, she walked toward Kim. She was wearing a plain T-shirt and nothing else. Melissa kept her distance, staying on the opposite side of the table. "We need to talk."

"I knew you would say that."

"Don't you agree?"

"Before you say anything, let me get this out." Kim turned, leaning against the counter and spreading both hands out. "I'm sorry I've been ignoring you. I know how hard this must be. But I need you to understand how I've made a lot of progress with Joshua and think I can wean him completely from the dolls."

"Do you mean that?" Although it was a relief to hear the accent lessening, Melissa thought of the mask in the dark the previous night as taking a small step back. It was the first time in her memory that she'd felt ashamed when she was with her girlfriend.

"I can't guarantee anything, but yes, I mean it."

"After that, what's your plan?"

"We have an aunt who lives downstate. I spoke with her the other day when you were at work. If Joshua doesn't object, I plan to drive him down once I think the time is right. Maybe we can talk him into staying with her or at least alternating between here and there." She paused, closing her eyes, looking as if she were summoning strength.

"Look, I know you disagree with how I'm handling this, but I don't know what else to do. When I take the dolls away, he has fits and refuses to eat. That's why we are always in the room. He is afraid to be more than a few feet from the dolls, and I know how much you detest them. I'm sure you can hear him crying through the walls. That's why I've been indulging him, even though I know better."

Melissa's eyebrow arched as the accent crept back in.

"I know how odd this's, but I'm not exactly an expert here at raising a mentally disturbed child." It took restraint to not immediately try to talk her into leaving all this madness behind.

Taking a deep breath, Melissa said, "I'm not trying to judge you and doing my best to be understanding here. But please, just stop alienating me. I can't take it anymore."

"I'm very sorry. I know I've been preoccupied." Kim looked away, her bottom lip trembling.

"I would use other terms rather than preoccupied to describe your recent behavior." Melissa ran her hand through her hair, fighting to let go of the anger and frustration that was consuming her. "Also, don't ever try what you did last night again."

Kim raised an eyebrow in confusion. "What're you talking about, Mel?"

Melissa knew Kim had to be embarrassed but couldn't believe she would lie. It was not in her to tell even a tiny white lie. Melissa's hand began to throb as she thought of what they had done. Confused by the earnest look on her partner's face, she thought it best to let it go for now. "Forget it. What can I do to help?"

Her lover's face was bunched, creating false wrinkles. "I wish I knew for sure. This's all so difficult." She wiped her nose with her sleeve. "All I do know is that Joshua wants nothing to do with you because he thinks we're sinnin'. And now, with all that he's got through, I didn't think it wise to try to force 'em to learn somethin' he don't really understand and been taught to hate."

Hearing every word accentuated with such a strong accent made Melisa cringe. "I can appreciate that. I really can, but you know I won't hide who we are. Not for anyone." *Even you.* The thought brought an even deeper emptiness.

Ignoring the comment, Kim continued. "Look, I was gonna make dinner for the three of us tonight. I don't wanta axe this, but I thought it would be a good first step if you're, ah. willin' to just act as friends in front of 'em."

There was a long silence as she contemplated her willingness and ability to fake her way through the evening. Melissa thought she could hear the sound of the sewing machine coming from the hallway again. Everything was moving too fast. Not knowing what else to do, she eventually said, "I might be willing to do that. As long as you promise, we are working to tell him the truth very soon."

Her eyes lit up. "You sure?"

Seeing some color in her girlfriend's face brought a tinge of hope. "Kim, I would do anything for you. If you think it will help, I promise not to say anything that would make him uncomfortable. If you promise to be working toward stopping all of those... behaviors."

"Thank you!" Kim's chapped lips erupted into a warm smile. "This'll get easier, real soon. I know it!"

Melissa hesitantly walked across the kitchen toward her girlfriend. She said in an unconvincing voice, "It will." Kim took a step forward and wrapped her arms around Melissa. She felt like an entirely different person, somehow less dense, and her typical sweet smell had been replaced with the smell of mothballs. Melissa tried not to let her mind run in a thousand directions and just ignore the impulse deep inside her, warning her to run.

The rain never let up. When Melissa returned after work, she made her way to the kitchen and the smell of pasta sauce. The garlic scent was so strong that she could almost taste the food.

Joshua sat at the table. His hair was combed, and it was the first time Melissa could remember him looking almost clean. He gave her a dull stare, his eyes glazed over as if he were on something. With a forced smile, she sat down and looked at Kim, who was at the counter, wearing a flared skirt, tight blouse, and heels. Swallowing hard as she tried to work through all of this, Melissa said, "Looks like you've had a busy afternoon. It smells great in here."

Kim turned, holding a salad bowl. Her face was covered in garish makeup; her lipstick was thick and uneven, and her eyes were darkly lined with so much mascara that it looked almost cartoonish. "Thank you. We've been cookin' fur hours."

It took effort not to scream out, *What's wrong with you!* Melissa slid her chair back until it bumped into the wall. Their calmness was striking every nerve. Adding to the sense of unease, Joshua lay something across her lap under the table.

She knew it was a mask the moment her fingertips made contact. He gave her a knowing smile as he leaned back in his chair. Remembering Kim saying how close she thought she was to getting through to Joshua, Melissa meekly asked, "Are we going to be eating soon?"

With a self-satisfied look, Kim asked, "Sure are. Can you lead us in prayer?"

"What?"

Joshua interrupted, his voice now in a high pitch. "Aren't we going to wait until we're all here, Kimmy?"

"Kim. What does that mean?" Melissa twitched at the sweat running down her sides as she desperately tried to make eye contact with her partner. "Who else is coming?"

"Ignore that." Kim's eyes darted to the hallway and then back to Melissa. "If you don't mind, can you please begin the prayer so we can start? I know it's not somethin' we're used to doin', but it's a tradition in *our* family."

The ridiculous charade was making her skin crawl. Struggling to compose herself, Melissa looked at the odd child to her right. His tongue was hanging between his plump lips, making her want to slap him for all he had done to her and Kim's relationship. It was the first time in her adult life that she'd had an impulse toward violence of any kind.

Kim sat compulsively arranging her skirt. "Can you please put on the mask first?"

Melissa looked at her girlfriend's smiling face as her heart skipped a beat and then suddenly raced to make up for the interruption, sending adrenaline coursing through her. "Kim, I'm trying to be understanding here, but please... don't ask me to do that."

Joshua looked at her and pleaded, "Please, Auntie Melissa, just for the prayer! Then we won't have any more masks this evenin', I promise, and besides, it'll make everything perfect for her arrival."

Melissa stared at Kim. Through her obscene makeup, she smiled encouragingly, subtly urging her on. Melissa thought about dashing out of the condo and never returning. The weight of the decision froze her. To buy a few seconds, Melissa reached beneath the table and grabbed the mask. The material was rough against her skin, reminding her of sandpaper rubbing against her flesh.

Breathing was now like sucking through a narrow straw. As she gasped for clean air, black dots floated in front of her face. Frantically, her mind raced, coating her in sweat. She desperately wanted to believe there was some reason just beyond her understanding that could explain all that was happening. There had to be a reason; her Kim was far too precious to be acting this way for no reason.

Just as she was making up her mind to bolt for the door, Joshua tugged at her sleeve and leaned closer. He smelled as if he hadn't bathed in some time.

"Put it on quick before Ma gets here, Auntie."

A slow, dragging sound came from the hallway. The noise was in competition with the thudding of Melisa's heart. She placed both hands on the table, wishing away the anxiety creeping through her, threatening her consciousness. As the noise grew, a shadow loomed across the floor.

Glancing to her right, she saw the life-sized doll enter the kitchen. In its mittened hand, it held a girl doll with black hair. Moving in an awkward, jerky motion, it sat at the head of the table.

Once settled, it turned its head deliberately toward Melissa. The shiny button eyes reflected the dim light of the kitchen. Wondering if she was possibly going insane, Melissa froze. Her blood felt like it was thickening and expanding in every vein. Her heart was beating so fast that she imagined it exploding, carrying her away from whatever madness she had walked into.

Watching at the abomination that was now taking the chair to her right, Melissa silently wished the panic would make her black out. The last bit of logic she had left was urging her to brush past the doll and run for the front door. Knowing she wouldn't make it, there was less than a few inches between the doll and the wall, she shifted her chair back as far as she could, waiting for the opportunity to bolt.

"Mel. Please put the mask on. Or do you need Mamma to help you?"

The thought of the hideous creature touching her was more than she could handle.

Shaking, she yanked the father mask on. The tight material limited her sightline, nearly cutting out her peripheral vision entirely. She stared at the top of Kim's head, watching as she bowed and joined hands with her brother. With her right hand, Kim reached out and took the doll's.

The mask was suffocating. She was sweating so profusely that the cloth was sticking to her face. Now that their new guest was fully seated, as Melissa was about to take the chance to run, the creature clamped down on her hand, the tufted fabric enveloping her fingers. The grip was like a steel clamp encased in cotton.

To her right, Joshua grabbed her opposite hand and squeezed tight. His palm was moist as he clenched much too hard. Trying to listen over his giggling, she heard Kim begin a short prayer. The woman she loved more than anything looked like a stranger as she recited long- forgotten words through her heavily painted lips.

After Kim finished, she raised her head, meeting Melissa's eyes inside the mask. "Welcome to something greater than yourself."

Feeling the doll frantically tug at her hand, Melissa squeezed back as hard as she could.

There was no resistance. Realizing that her suspicion was accurate—there was no one inside what she desperately needed to believe was only a costume—she fought the urge to relieve herself.

As she squirmed away from both, what she now believed was their mother and Joshua, the mask tightened as it joined with her skin. The dirty cloth weaving into her flesh was like pins being driven deep into her nerve endings. "Please, Kim! I love you so much! Whatever this is, help me." Her flesh was opening, the pain shooting through her in waves.

Knowing now she was completely on her own, with an effort, she pulled away from Joshua and grasped frantically at the bottom of the mask with her free hand. The worn material wouldn't budge, as it melded with her flesh.

Panic heated her face as she desperately tugged at the tattered cloth. It was like trying to yank hair from her head. Each movement brought agonizing pain, reminding her of pulling a Band-Aid from a bleeding scab.

Darkness enveloped her as the fabric began closing over her eyes, leaving only the tiny spaces of the buttonholes to stare through. When the mother doll pushed her chair away and tugged Melissa firmly onto her lap, Melissa writhed as she felt the doll's hand viciously strike her behind.

Humming, Kim and Joshua came and stood on each side as the mother doll administered the punishment. Melissa's frantic screams were stifled by the rigid stitching of the cloth, the mouth closing over her lips, as she began to understand her place in her new family.

TREATS

I t was just getting dark when the doorbell rang. Tobi walked
to the foyer after disentangling himself from helping his
eight-year-old get into his ninja turtle costume. As the door
opened, a gust of wind scattered a few random leaves across his
foyer. The air was cold but had a hint of humidity in it.

Standing under the dim light of the single bulb on his porch
was a skeleton that had to be at least six feet tall. The costume
was so detailed that it looked like it had come from a movie. It
had fully articulated bones that appeared to float in space. Each
one looked three-dimensional.

Cleverly, they'd concealed the black suit that had to be
covering the trick-or-treater's body.

Tobi, already frustrated by the very long day, said sarcasti-
cally, "Aren't you a little old for trick-or-treating?"

The skeleton stood unmoving.

Tobi turned his head sideways, examining the costume and
trying to figure out how it could look hollow in the center. The
skeletal face tilted to the side, mimicking him. Somehow, the
eye sockets looked empty, revealing blacked-out holes where the
eyes should be.

Tobi heard his boy whine in the background. "Help us with our costumes! It's getting soooo late!"

With a sigh, Tobi grabbed a bite-sized Snickers and tossed it toward the dirty sack the skeleton held at his side. With a flick of the wrist, the trick or treater awkwardly yanked the sack backward, letting the candy fall to the ground. Catching the light, Tobi saw that the wrinkled bag was wet and stained the color of crimson. The skeletal creature, now still, continued his vacant stare. His bottom jaw moved erratically, making an odd clicking noise. After a few seconds, in a jerky motion, as if it took great effort, it raised its arm and lifted the dirty pillowcase at chest level.

"All right, pal, suit yourself." He stepped back to close the door. The skeleton lifted the sack higher and, with its other hand, dug inside, finally pulling out a plastic toy the size of a paperback book. It was a very detailed replica of a haunted house with cobwebs and ghosts in each window.

Tobi took a half step back, staring beyond the skeleton to see whether a group of his friends was putting him up to the bizarre show. Not only was the leaf-covered walkway empty, but the street and surrounding sidewalks were also empty. Just a minute ago, the neighborhood was a kinetic whirl of activity. It was as if the strange visitor had swallowed up all the fun in the surrounding darkness.

The sense that something was very off about this creature brought dread that crept through Tobi, bringing tightness to his chest. The feeling clung to him like a wet blanket. Something deep inside told him this wasn't just some odd teenager's attempt at a joke. His stomach muscles tightened as he watched the skeleton caress its dated toy.

With a long, thin finger, the shadow creature pressed a button at the top of the well-worn decoration. The trigger lit up the windows with a dull light from inside, and organ music came from an unseen monotone speaker.

After several flashes, a hoarse voice creaked out, "Trick or treat." The digitized words held menace as if they were a demand, not a cherished childish intonation.

Tobi stared at the creature that his imagination was trying to convince him that he wasn't a man. His breathing tightened and sweat began to run down his sides. Even in his fear, politeness almost made him retrieve another piece of candy from the bowl, hoping the act would make him leave without confrontation. In the background, he could hear his children whine and bicker. The noises sounded like they were miles away. Frozen, he tried to process what this very tall kid was up to.

The skeletal hand moved forward nearer to Tobi's face, and the button was tapped again.

This close, it smelled dirty, reminding Tobi of the outhouse behind his uncle's shed up north.

The recorded organ played the same dreary tune, followed by the "Trick or Treat" demand. Both the tune and noise held the grainy quality of a vinyl album.

Tobi hunched his shoulders, pulling his head closer to his body, trying to make himself smaller—a well-practiced defense mechanism for a man who had been forced to physically defend himself from a very early age.

"I don't know what you want. Please, just go." The weakness in his voice this near to his family brought deep shame. It was a betrayal to the facade he'd spent so much time cultivating— that of the brave father and husband, not the coward who let everyone walk all over him, which was just under the surface.

The skeleton moved slightly forward, taking a hesitant step toward the house. His bones jangled, making it look as if the creature were seconds away from falling into pieces. Making a guttural moan, the skull, in unison with its spindly fingers, emphatically bobbed the toy in Tobi's direction, desperately urging his attention to it. "Trick or treat" once again echoed from the plastic house. As the button was frantically pressed, the words began slurring as if the batteries were wearing down.

Despite his fear, wanting to be rid of him, Tobi foolishly whispered "Treat?" while staring into the shadows that should contain eyes.

The skeleton nodded in a single abrupt nod, the porch light dancing along its graying surface. In a jerky motion, the hand holding the toy went slowly back into the bag. After a few seconds, it came back out, holding something the size and shape of a mini sausage wrapped in cloth, the ends held together with loosely tied strings.

The skeletal head nodded as its hand thrust forward, miming for Tobi to take the treat.

Tobi tugged at the offering with the very tips of his fingers, carefully avoiding the hand that was inches from his own, as if it were diseased. Gripping it, he felt that the treat was warm and damp, making him flinch.

The second the gift was exchanged, the skeleton turned, walking away. Its movements looked like the old Claymation figures from a Ray Harryhausen film. Each labored movement flashing forward shaky inches at a time, as if caught in suspended animation. With an unsteady hand, it waved over its shoulder without looking back.

Tobi slammed the door shut and peered through the sidelight. With only the dull bulb from the porch, the skeleton was no longer visible. All Tobi saw now was the last few leaves on his lawn dancing from the harsh wind wiping across shadows. With the door closed, it was like a great weight had been removed from his chest.

As he turned back into his foyer, unsure if he should laugh or cry, he glanced down at the treat in his hand. He glared at it as if it were a hairy spider crawling up his arm. Tobi thought about throwing it in the trash and forgetting the whole encounter, but something compelled him to open it.

Just as he tugged at the frayed string, Steven screamed, pulling Tobi from his momentary trance. Glancing into the great room, his daughter was pulling his son's turtle mask over her head, giving her the appearance of a reptilian fairy princess.

"Emily, give that back!" With his tiny fists clenched, Steven knocked over the much- shorter girl who was half his age, and then the hysterics began.

Coming down the hallway, his wife Kaye entered the room with her blonde hair in tight curls. She was wearing a white tunic stretched across her enormous belly. With her eyes wide, she looked at her husband with the familiar "Can't you keep them in line for even a few minutes?" look. It was a favorite of hers lately, coming in second only with the comments that he was never present and that he'd better start soon.

"Emily, shut off the waterworks, and give your brother his mask now!" Kaye stood with her hands on her hips, in her classic mother pose, waiting for the fight.

"But he hit me!"

"Now! Or no trick-or-treating!"

The whining instantly stopped as they, in unison, looked to their mother, shocked by the threat. Emily rolled as she sat up, taking off the mask and tossing it to her older brother with an angelic smile. She whispered, "Here ya go, stupid!"

With order restored, Tobi, still slightly disoriented, shoved the small package from the night visitor into the front pocket of his pants. Nothing felt right. He was still foggy like he'd just been pulled from a dream, but he was getting somewhat calmer. The children, thankfully, brought him back to reality as they usually did. A reality where he was ready to convince himself that the skeleton was just some odd joke, as he'd first suspected.

Kaye turned, placing her hand on the cheap-looking laser pistol that hung from the holster on her belt. "So, what do you think of pregnant Leia?" She let out a robust laugh.

Tobi said quietly, "You look great."

She did, even at eight months pregnant. Then again, she always did. It was what caused so much tension between them. The always-perfect wife married the man who was barely keeping them afloat.

"Is it cold outside?"

"It's not bad."

"Good. I hate when the kids wear jackets that cover their costumes." She turned, grabbing plastic bags from the couch. "All right, munchkins, are you ready to get some loot?"

"Yeah!" was yelled in unison.

Tobi wanted to ask whether they could wait a few minutes, thinking of the skeleton, but bit it back. Keeping it to himself made the experience feel less real.

Grunting, Kaye pulled on her sandals. They were the only shoes that fit since her feet began swelling. "You sure you can't come with?"

He didn't want to be alone, but had no choice. "We've been through this. Rick moved the meeting to the first thing in the morning. I have to get the presentation ready."

"Of course you do. Wouldn't want to disappoint... him." Her smile turned quickly to a frown. "All right then." She walked by Tobi with a disappointed look that was growing more frequent whenever they spoke. Since his promotion over a year ago, which brought in very little extra money but demanded far more of his time, the tension between them was getting out of control, making Tobi obsessively question whether the unexpected pregnancy was the only thing keeping them together.

With the kids trailing behind, they made it to the tight foyer. When the door opened, for an instant, Tobi thought for sure the skeleton would still be there—getting ready to jump in front of his family from the shadows. A wave of relief coursed through him when he saw only the darkness of the night awaiting them.

"Have fun, guys."

Emily turned back. "We will, Daddy. Please don't miss us too much. Okay?"

Tobi smiled at the earnestness in his youngest's voice. He watched them walk down the front path to the sidewalk, fighting the urge to blow off work and enjoy the night. Knowing he didn't have it in him to shirk his responsibility, he leaned against the door jamb with a sigh.

The street was once again alive with costumed children chattering and yelling way too loudly, fueled by their quest for more sugar. Knowing he had to get moving, he grabbed the candy bowl from the tiny table in the foyer and left it on the front stoop next to the carved pumpkins, grabbing the sign he'd written earlier. In bold magic marker, it read, "Please take only one piece! Happy Halloween!"

The candles in the jack-o'-lanterns flickered across the words. Although he knew the first group of teenagers who came by would empty the bowl, he couldn't afford the distraction of running to the door every five minutes. Looking down the street, he saw his family go to the first house. There was some disappointment that they could look so happy without him there.

He slowly closed the door and went down the hallway to the spare bedroom he used as a makeshift office. Before he sat at his computer, he fished the package from the skeleton out of his pocket and tossed it in the trash.

***

After nearly 15 minutes of unproductive work, he stared down into the waste pail. The thought of what the skeleton had given him was like an earworm burrowing deeper and deeper.

After retyping the same unintelligible sentence for the fourth time, he finally rolled his chair back.

Bending down, he pulled the wrapper from the odd treat using his thumb and forefinger.

Inspecting it inches from his face, the outer material felt like soft leather. As he tugged at the moist strings, something deep in his brain screamed for him to stop, but curiosity won out. With the strings off, he slowly rolled the tiny package open.

Inside was what resembled a bloody tongue. Trying to identify what it was, he brought it to his nose, and the rancid odor made him recoil. Shaking his head to make the smell go away, he glimpsed the handwriting inside the worn wrapper. Smoothing it out, he read:

Finish your treat. If you don't, you will be sorry.

Tobi let out a nervous chuckle. The awkward laughter sounded out of place in the darkness. Reluctantly, with his finger, he pressed the sinewy material. It recoiled, feeling like compressed jelly.

Placing it back on the top of the trash, he thought of calling the police or at least posting on his neighborhood watch's website but decided not to. Whoever came up with the elaborate joke would eventually reveal themselves, and when they did, he wouldn't give them the satisfaction of showing that he was shaken.

He let out a deep sigh, trying to shake the sense that this was a warning, when his phone rang, piercing the silence. A warning bell chimed inside. It was the same feeling he had when he heard a strange noise in the middle of the night, making it a struggle to reconcile it and use logic to stay calm.

Anxiously, he pulled out the phone from his pants pocket. The call was from Kaye. *You didn't finish your treat; now, here's the penance.*

Shaking the horrible thought from his head, full of trepidation, he conjured the strength he didn't know he had and answered.

"Tobi?" It wasn't his wife's voice. The cadence was familiar, but he couldn't quite place it.

His eyebrow twitched. *The treat was an omen. You know it.* "Ah, yes..."

"It's Madeline. I live in the colonial brick house by the ravine. We met at the Bakers' barbecue, remember? I... well... don't know how else to say this. Umm, this is awkward, but there's a... problem. Kaye isn't feeling well."

He cut her off. "Is it the baby?"

"Well, we aren't sure. She's sitting on my couch right now." There was a shuffling sound. "She's having what I guess you could say are irregular heartbeats. We called an ambulance, Tobi."

Finish your treat. If you don't, you will be sorry. His eyes flashed to the waste pail, his head filling with images of the skeleton. *That was no costume.* "Is she going to be all right?"

"I really can't say. She's in noticeable pain."

You will be sorry. "Where are the children?"

"They're in the kitchen with Dan, my husband. Tobi, I think you'd better get here right away." There was a loud scraping noise before she whispered, "I just walked away far enough so she can't hear me. It's bad, Tobi, really bad. She was standing on the porch laughing, and then a second later, it was like a lightning bolt hit her. I've never seen anything like it."

Her tone made his chest ache. "What's your address?" His eyes darted to the garbage again, glaring at the open wrapper with the cryptic message taunting him. Electricity tingled his skin as he tried to hold onto the phone.

Just eat it; keep her and the baby safe.

Bile rose in his throat, staring at the slimy grotesque treat. His immediate thoughts were elsewhere, but some base instinct recognized the address. Mumbling, "I'll be right there," his stomach dropped.

Tossing the phone onto the desk, his legs felt like they could no longer hold him. Leaning forward for stability, he gripped the cold surface and gasped into the darkness.

"Oh, God! Please, not the baby!" Reason was rapidly evaporating as he thought of their unborn child.

Just eat it, or you will be sorry...

With the back of his hand, he wiped at his mouth, his skin getting caught on the stubble as his mind raced. He reached into the trash and took out the offering from the skeleton, making his stomach rumble. The cold, soggy mess contoured his hand.

"This can't be happening."

But it is.

The strain was making his lips quiver. *What could it hurt to just eat the thing?*

Knowing he couldn't live with the doubt a second longer, he shoved the entire piece of what he hoped was meat into his mouth at once, violently chewing the spongy treat and trying to ignore the rancid taste and smell. Beginning to swallow, instantly, his throat tried to regurgitate whatever he had just consumed, causing him to dry heave. In seconds, the barely chewed mystery treat got lodged in his throat.

Coughing and wheezing, with the realization that no air would pass and that there was no one around to help him, his eyes watered. Panic seized him. Fighting to swallow, the obstruction would neither go up nor down, stealing his breath. Claustrophobia crept into every muscle as he slapped at his throat. Finally, in a violent spasm, the chunk dislodged, sliding down.

Gagging, he reached for the coffee cup next to his computer. Realizing it was empty, he spit into it, trying to rid himself of the awful taste. It brought a phantom memory of when his grandmother had forced him to eat partially cooked chicken gizzards to teach him a lesson about appreciating food. The memory increased the anguish of having an unknown substance in his stomach.

He flinched as his phone rattled, and a text message from Kaye appeared. With his eyes stinging from the aftertaste, he swiped up the phone. There was a picture of his kids in their costumes, holding plastic bags with stencils of a haunted house printed on them. Beneath the photo was the caption "Too much candy!" in bold lettering.

It's real. The warning was real; you saved them. Hyperventilating, Tobi frantically hit the call button, considering that maybe this was just a delayed text and not proof of the skeleton's power.

A heaving voice said, "Hello."

"Kaye?"

"No, it's not Kaye."

Tobi's heart paused as he waited for Madeline to ask why he was calling back instead of rushing over.

"It's Princess Leia." She let out her throaty laugh.

Tobi, despite his fear, could picture her oversized belly dancing in the white tunic she was wearing. For the first time in what felt like a year, it seemed like he could get enough air into his lungs to stay upright. "Are you okay?"

"Yeah, why wouldn't I be? I'm not that fat yet. Although I wish I could've worn my gym shoes instead of these dumbass sandals. My dogs are barking!"

"Didn't you just have Madeline call me?"

"All right, seriously, what's up with you? You drinking? Who's Madeline?"

Tobi became dizzy, so dizzy that he laid his head against the desktop as squiggly lines floated across his eyes. He didn't know if it was from what he ate or relief.

Maybe they're all in on it, and you fell for it, eating that disgusting hunk of flesh.

Tobi knew Kaye had been unhappy for some time, but it was hard to accept that she would do something like this to him. "Nothing, ignore me."

"Ooookay."

In the background, the kids were screaming. "Let's go, Mom! It's getting late."

Kaye yelled back, "Hold your horses; there's plenty of time. Tobi, seriously, what's going on with you?"

Although he needed to know what he just ate, he wouldn't give her the satisfaction of knowing how gullible he was. "Nothing. I'll see you when you get back."

"Okay, it should be around another half hour. By then, our little turtle and princess will be worn out."

Before he could respond, the doorbell rang twice in quick succession. He looked toward the dark hallway, saying, "See you then." The words were a whisper.

Seconds later, the door opened, followed by the waning sound of organ music coming from the living room. After a crackle of synthetic thunder, there was the hoarse voice saying once again, "Trick or treat."

He knew he'd locked the door; he was sure of it. Using the desk for support, he inched his way to a standing position. Looking at the baseball bats in the corner, he thought better than to arm himself. The anger was too great. Slowly, with his legs shuffling across the hardwood floor, he made his way to the main room.

It was dark except for the light coming from the foyer, creating odd silhouettes. Standing in the middle of the room was his tormentor. He held his dirty sack at his side and the plastic toy in his thin fingers.

Slowly, it dropped the bag and waved Tobi to it with its index finger, moving in rhythmic motion. Clicking on the light, Tobi lost all doubt. This was no trick. On this sacred night, the dead had come to visit him. A wave of cold settled into his bones, making him shiver. With no shadows to hide behind, he could see through the center of the hideous being.

"Please leave."

His request was met with the finger moving more rapidly, beckoning him closer. Feeling like someone was stabbing him with needles, Tobi slowly moved backward. The skeleton lurched forward and took Tobi's hand, clenching it with what felt like a vise. In swift motion, Toby's fingers were raised to its exposed teeth, and the flesh was pierced with a flicking motion. Shock froze him in place.

Like a baby on a bottle, it sucked, pulling blood. The veins in Toby's arm swelled and ached as the skeleton sucked life from him. The blood, having no throat to guide it, trickled down the spine and oozed into the ribcage. The red liquid seemed to awaken something. The bones absorbed it, making the creature appear more whole.

After nearly a half minute, the skeleton let go of its grip and sat down on the couch, no longer in awkward jerking motions. Tobi tugged at his aching finger, willing the skeleton away with his stare.

The odd creature did not budge. It just stood stock-still with its head tilted slightly upward, glaring up at Tobi.

Consumed with fury, thinking of all the hideous creature had put him through, Tobi leaned forward, grabbed the skeleton's wrist, intent on throwing him out the door, and screamed, "Why are you doing this?"

With a tug, the entire arm came loose at the shoulder. The lack of resistance caused Tobi to lose his balance, sending him toppling over the coffee table into the designer chair. Repulsed, he thrust the appendage onto his lap. As soon as it was free of his grip, it slithered like a snake, the fingers leading the way until they were around his neck and tightened with remarkable strength. With its other hand, the skeleton grabbed the haunted house toy, lifting it onto the arm of the couch, and pressed the button. This time, after the foreboding organ and thunder, the incantation changed. "Thank you for the nourishment."

Tobi spat and coughed, fighting desperately to get free of the grip. "What did you make me eat?" The words brought the after-taste of the spongy substance.

"That was all that was left of my human form."

"*Why?*"

"You chose my treat as a trade-off."

"For what?"

"For your wife's and children's lives. You see, it was necessary, as I needed a host to begin my transformation."

Realizing his place in the bizarre ritual, Tobi tried to scream, causing the skeleton to snap its fingers, making the hand around his throat tighten. Choking, Tobi fought against the darkness that was coming over him.

The skeleton pressed the button on top of the toy once more. As the organ music played, he snapped its fingers again, and the grip loosened. "Do not make me do that again."

The room became eerily silent as the skeleton made a gazeless stare. Inclining its head slightly toward the plastic facade, the words pierced the silence. "You must now choose."

Tobi, trying desperately to release the grip from the hand at his throat, croaked out, "Choose what?"

"The unborn child or its father's life."

The words struck like bullets hitting deep inside him. He leaned forward, becoming disorientated. Fear was choking out logic. All he knew now was what he felt. His life had passed a boundary of reason to a place where a skeleton could control everything. Weeping, he muttered, "Please. Please, no."

"We haven't much time. I still have work to do tonight."

Tobi stared at the unfeeling demon that sat before him. His mind was racing, trying to find a way out. Glaring at the fireplace poker to his right, as if the skeleton could read his mind, the fingers surrounding his throat tightened and the house said "No" in its electronic cadence.

Defeated, Tobi squeaked out, "Don't harm the baby!"

"You're sure?"

"Yes." The fear was turning to anger as he struggled against the claw-like hand bruising his throat.

"It will be done before the evening is over." The skeleton snapped its fingers, and this time, the arm slithered away, back to the skeleton. With a sickening noise, it reattached itself, making the gruesome creature whole once again. Slowly, it grabbed its plastic toy from the couch and lovingly placed it back into the sack.

The skeleton stood, and then, with a quick nod of his bare skull, sauntered toward the front door. As the door slammed, Tobi thought about chasing the creature, but he knew it was useless. What was done was done.

Less than 20 minutes later, Kaye came back with the kids. Tobi had no idea how long it would take the skeletal visitor to collect its dark debt. He chose to make his last minutes as pleasant as he could. He spent the next hour feeling like he was strapped to a bomb, every second filled with fear, loathing, and doubt. Like a zombie, he went along his nightly routine, trying to pretend none of this had taken place.

As he put the children to bed, he kissed them for what he assumed was the final time. The sadness was so deep that he eventually felt nothing more than a dull ache from shock. After watching them sleep for a while, he made it to his own bed. He looked at Kaye and had so many things to say that he couldn't control his tongue.

He wanted to clear the air and leave, having made sure she wouldn't carry any guilt for who they'd become over the last year with the strain of children, financial burdens, and an unexpected child on the way. When he opened his mouth, Tobi's lip quivered so violently that he bit his fist to stop himself from weeping uncontrollably.

As he was about to speak, the house phone rang. The voice on the other end was his sister-in-law. "Tobi, are you there?"

The concern in her tone made his stomach turn. "Yes ... Trish, what is it?"

"Tobi, it's your brother. Something terrible has happened."

"*What is it?*"

"He took the dog for a walk, and some type of animal tore him limb from limb." There was a long sobbing cry. "The police said most of his skin is gone."

Tobi, wondering what was happening to his family, asked, "How bad is he?"

"I don't think he's going to make it to the hospital." Tobi could hear his nephew's barking questions at their mother in the background. "I can't handle this. I need you here to help make ... decisions."

"Where are you?"

"Following the ambulance to Mercy." Kaye grabbed his arm. "What's going on?"

"It's Hal. He was attacked." He grabbed her hand. "It doesn't look like he is going to make it."

Kaye let out a shrill cry, grabbing her belly. "No, no, how can this be? What about—" Tears streamed from her face as she rocked back and forth, cradling her belly.

As Tobi glared at her, he recognized guilt in her stare. The voice of the skeleton echoed in his head:

... or the baby's father.

He slapped his hand to his mouth, holding back the words that would confirm what he didn't want to believe. Filled with disgusted relief, he got off the bed and glared at Kaye. She lay face down, using the pillows to stifle her sobs.

Tobi began pacing, wanting equally to leave and hug his wife.

The doorbell rang twice. It was like a hypnotist's bell. In a trance, he walked to the front door. He opened it slowly, knowing what he was going to see. Standing before him was the skeleton draped in his brother's skin. The stained flesh sagging, giving the appearance of a demented doll. This time, it didn't bother with the plastic toy. It simply reached into the sack, pulling out a treat.

Tobi reached for the disgusting cloth. After delivering its gift, the skeleton slowly walked away, its new skin sagging and rolling with each measured step as it disappeared into the darkness.

When the door was closed, Tobi quickly unwrapped the unwanted gift. When the strings came off, he fought to control his breathing. He stared down into his palms, not believing what he clearly saw. Once again, there was a handwritten message on the inside of the wrapper.

See you next year.

NEXT IN LINE

Robert stood at the entrance to the Alien Experience, completely unaware that he was about to cross a void between time and space. The sign advertising the close encounter had a retro flying saucer. It was in the hallway of Corridor A, behind the rows of exhibitors' tables, that made up Artist's Alley. The annual comic book and collectible convention known as Collectecon was the fourth largest of its kind that came through the northern Chicago suburb in the town of New Bremen.

Not having the funding of the major conventions, the guest list was comprised of no more than C-level celebrities. Most were unrecognizable former performers, who mostly stared longingly for a passing visitor to pay for a signed headshot. Even without the draw of the really big names, there was still quite a turnout every year. With lower admission fees, it was easier to lure in choice store owners, those who understood the appeal of their unique merchandise. The passion of their clients gave the show the well-deserved moniker as an expert's convention.

It was Sunday, midafternoon, and Robert had only one more panel to attend to reap the full benefits of his expensive three-day VIP pass, which entitled him to early entry and exclusive access. In between the previous sessions, he'd been over every table in the grand concourse twice and considered finding a quiet place to take a short nap to kill the nearly two-hour wait before the *Space Coast* cast would gather in Conference Room Eight. While he was contemplating sleep versus spending 20 bucks on the unknown attraction, a shapely female alien approached him. She wore brilliant silver shorts with suspenders over a white, almost transparent leotard.

The barker flashed him a bright smile. "Welcome to our transportation module, Robert."

He was so taken aback by the woman's eyes that he almost didn't question how she knew his name. They were the size and shape of pears, only black and reflective. As he stared at his image on their surface, he was amazed at how well the alien eyes blended into the surrounding skin.

He muttered almost to himself, "Do I know you?"

The alien smiled. She had very human lips that puckered as she pointed with an extra- long index finger to Robert's badge, which dangled on his chest from his lanyard.

Feeling foolish, he smiled awkwardly. "Oh."

"Well? Are you here today to be part of the alien experience?"

"What is it ... exactly?"

"If you're brave enough, we will bring you aboard our vessel, and you will experience a dramatic launch to our world in the cosmos!"

"So, is it a simulation ride?"

"I believe you will find it stimulating, Robert."

He didn't know if she was playing a part or just that dense. It didn't seem at all likely that anyone here could be, but you never knew. "How long does it take?"

"Ten of your Earth minutes."

Thinking that's two bucks a minute, pretty steep after all the money he'd already put out, he said, "How long is the wait?"

Looking past her, he could see a few people bunched in a tight line through the angled hallway entrance. A wall obscured how many others actually stood in front of the small group.

"The wait varies on the frequency of the launching of our space modules." The alien host placed her finger on her earpiece and whispered in a foreign language. With a nod, she said, "As of right now, it should be no longer than half an hour, assuming the ship returns in good condition from the previous launch." The wicked smile was back.

Knowing he probably couldn't sleep anyway, as being around this many people always energized him, Robert fished through his cargo pants and reluctantly pulled out a tangled wad of singles left over from his various purchases throughout the weekend. As he was counting out the money, his overburdened backpack slipped off his shoulder. Before it reached his elbow, the alien girl, in a flash, grabbed it and handed it back to him. As he slipped the strap back on his shoulder, he quietly said, "Thank you." Wondering how she had reflexes like that, he handed her the money, feeling slightly uneasy, as if he'd witnessed something he shouldn't have.

Smiling, she took the payment and stepped sideways, giving him just enough space to enter the narrow opening. As he passed, she said, "I hope you enjoy your experience, Robert."

The hallway was dark and narrow and took a right angle about 10 feet from where he stood. Filling that space were several other conventioneers, all with the same expression of blissful wariness. In the partially exposed space, the temperature was several degrees warmer, and there was an overwhelming odor coming from the concession booth back in Corridor A. Robert looked at his phone. There were no messages. He double-checked his alarm, which was still set for 3:40. That would give him plenty of time to get a good seat for his panel, regardless of what he did after whatever he'd just paid twenty bucks for was over.

He pulled his backpack forward and dug out the colored flyer for Collectecon. Interested primarily in the map to find the quickest path to his next stop, he unfolded the brochure. Finding the Artist's Alley, he used his finger to trace the hallway, discovering something very odd. All he saw was a restroom, and then the connection over the escalator to Concourse B. He turned his head sideways to make sure he wasn't disoriented. Either way he looked at it, his current location did not exist, or at least it didn't in the cheap handout.

Not overthinking the omission, he shoved the brochure into his backpack and walked the few feet forward that the line now afforded. As he caught up to a tall guy with amazingly long hair in a worn jean jacket, Robert heard shuffling from behind him. Dressed in a hooded, long- sleeve red T-shirt and black leggings was a raven-haired woman. Robert flashed a smile and then quickly looked forward, avoiding eye contact.

Pretty women always made him uneasy. On cue, his heart raced, and then he felt heat in his face. Focusing on the StratX music that he could barely hear over the hum of a thousand voices from the main room, he did his best to breathe. It was proving difficult in the stagnant air of the ventless hallway. The track from the hairband was screaming about "understanding their love" when a loud boom rang throughout the space. It was loud enough that it felt tangible, reminding him of the planes he used to watch fly over Lake Michigan at the Air and Water Show. Wondering what type of sound system this cheap outfit had on the other side of the wall, he heard the woman behind him speak in a much too loud voice.

"What the crap was that?"

Robert turned around, his backpack almost smacking her in the face. Feeling instantly less shy as he saw her covering her ears with her long nails, making her elbows point out, he responded, "Subwoofer must be right against the wall."

"Why does a spaceship need a subwoofer?" She let her arms fall before smiling and letting out a quick laugh. "You really thought about that, didn't you?" She gave him a playful push to his shoulder. She had to stretch to do it. Her head was well below Robert's chin.

"Yes, very funny."

"What is this anyway? I couldn't get anything out of the alien Barbie doll with big eyes. She is totally method with her demeanor and line delivery."

"I'm not sure. Some type of flight simulator, maybe?"

"So, you're like me. You thought the sign looked cool and figured what the hey." Putting her hand forward the old-fashioned way with her fingers hanging down, she said, "My name is Molly. Nice to meet you."

Not sure if she was expecting him to kiss the back of her hand or shake it, he weakly grabbed her fingers and gave them a half-shake. "Robert."

"So, I see you're one of the serious ones." She pointed at his lanyard. "I just came today. Mostly for the toy tables. I just headed in here to get away from the noise for a few minutes. This place is crazy nuts for a Sunday. Must have been complete bananas yesterday."

For one of the first times he could remember, Robert felt nearly completely calm as he spoke to a member of the opposite sex. Not wanting to analyze that too much and mess it up, he said, "Yeah, yesterday was swamped. You could barely make it down the aisles."

"That's the worst! It's the main reason I stopped cosplaying. Rubber outfits in barely air-conditioned rooms in a crowd of not-quite-normal comic collectors are not a good combo. Hey, pay attention." She nodded, looking past Robert.

He felt a flash of guilt, thinking she'd noticed his gaze going to her chest—he couldn't help it after she'd mentioned cosplay—before he realized the line behind him had disappeared. He took a few steps before coming to the turn in the hallway. Looking past the long-haired guy, he saw a small maze of a line that snaked up and down. Corded red velvet ropes separated the four rows of conventioneers in the rectangular room. As he looked across the sea of T-shirts, costumes, and ironic hats, he felt Molly come up next to him, her shoulder brushing the flannel of his sleeve.

"Not cutting, just figured it would be easier to talk this way. That is, if you want to. I don't want to be like one of those super-annoying unaware people on a plane who starts blabbing when everyone else is just like, 'Shut the eff up, man!'"

She smiled, and Robert's heartbeat went up. "No, it's cool. I like talking."

"Ha! Nerd!" She bumped him with her hip. "Just teasing. You've got to admit, that was just a really funny way to say that though."

Robert gave her a smirk. "Yeah, I guess it was."

"So, where're you from?"

"New Bremen."

"Cool, short drive then. I'm a city girl myself. I'm here mainly for Beanie Babies. I know, I know, they're lame, but I can't seem to get enough of them." She wrinkled her nose before continuing. "Okay, so I told my first lie. I do like Beanie Babies, but my real passion is *Archie* comics."

"Why would you lie about that?"

"Because I'm twenty-four and should have outgrown them a decade ago."

"Well, I'm twenty-eight and still read comics."

"Sure, but probably graphic novels and other cool crapola guys like you are into."

Even if the comment wasn't exactly directed at him, it was the first time that the word "cool" was part of anything he ever did. "Some of that, but I go vintage too." He wanted to tell her about the *Casper* series he had in his backpack, but thought it better to not quite let that out yet. He didn't want to challenge his cool status. Quickly changing the subject, he said, "Do you really like Beanie Babies?"

"Yup! My collection is small, but I like to believe it's significant." She let out a whisper of a laugh. "Right now, I'm waitressing, so I have to be very selective. That is, until I finish school."

"Where do you go to school?"

"Nowhere… yet. I guess that sounds kinda dumb out loud, but it's all part of my plan. First, I finished high school, S! That was the worst. Second, take eight years off and find myself, and then go to college knowing what I really want to do. I look at it as a reverse-retirement plan. If you think about it, it makes a lot of sense. When you're young and dumb, why not make the most of those years?"

The project engineer, who detested his job, nodded and wished he had the courage to live that way. A compulsive need to follow rules would never allow it, but it was a nice dream. The line moved forward a few more feet, bringing them close to the first turnstile. Seconds later, the boom came again, making him flinch. On this side of the hallway, it was slightly less significant, but it still brought a collective gasp from the group.

"How long have we been waiting? It feels like an hour." Her eyelashes flickered rapidly. "Oh, don't take that personally. I'm really having a lot of fun talking to you, but how long can this line be? If they're going to make you wait this long, they really should add more lights back here. It's kinda creepy, man, and not the good kind."

Robert looked at his phone. More than half an hour had gone by since the last time he'd checked. He was amazed, as it felt more like minutes. "About half an hour."

He looked back. There was no one behind them, not a single new interested visitor. "I would have to think we should be very close now." He stood on his toes and peered over the long haired man in his jean jacket, even leaning to the side. All he could see was blackness around the next corner.

"Yeah, you're probably right. Sorry, I wasn't trying to sound bitchy. I just don't like dark rooms with strangers. The smell in here doesn't help much either. It's the perfect mixture of farts and onions."

In the line to their right, an extremely overweight goateed man in a T-shirt that was two sizes too small for him laughed, looking

Molly up and down. Instinctively, Robert stepped in front of her, obscuring the view. "So, when your plan comes to fruition, what will you be studying?"

"What plan? Oh! No clue, dude, but that's by design. I refuse to think about it until my experimental phase is over. You see, this way, I won't contaminate my mind thinking about what I'm going to do instead of doing things I want to do right now."

"I can understand that." It was completely unlike his own thought process, but his response wasn't a lie. There was an odd logic in her plan.

"How about you? What do you do? I hate that phrase, 'do you do,' yet I always find myself using it, I guess, because it is so apropos."

"My job is boring. I don't like to talk about it." Robert always found it depressing to talk about his work on weekends. Even thinking about it felt like a betrayal of his limited free time.

"That's cool. Unless you're like a serial killer in disguise. In that case, I must insist you tell me."

The mischievous look in her eyes brought a tenderness he hadn't experienced before. Pulling him from the growing adulation, a voice full of static filled the room. Several of the conventioneers looked around the black fabric walls for the source.

"Attention, travelers. Sorry for the delay caused by our last launch. Our technicians have identified the issue, and our vessel is once again sound for takeoff. Boarding will resume immediately."

Robert glanced at his phone. Twenty more minutes had gone by. Assuming his phone had a glitch, he checked and saw that he had a full signal. Not knowing what else to do, he restarted it. As the hourglass flipped over endlessly, the booming noise once again reverberated throughout the waiting area. This time, it was even louder, causing Molly to jump. Instinctively, Robert flinched and pulled his arm back, allowing her space to lean against him, resulting in an unplanned hug. Her warmth made him tingle.

Without speaking, they smiled at one another. This close, he saw a small tattoo on the side of her neck—a butterfly inside a pair of inverted triangles. The impromptu embrace ended abruptly when the alarm on his phone went off. Silently, Molly used the noise as a cue to take a step back. Robert was thinking that what had just happened was a perfect moment, one of those unbelievable movie moments, or at least could have been if he'd only had the guts to lean in and kiss her. Instead, Robert smiled and entered the passcode, shutting off the alarm. His phone said an hour and forty minutes had passed. Assuming there was something wrong with the clock, he put the phone back into his pocket.

Molly rubbed her ears. "Whoever owns this contraption should really look into handing out earplugs if they're going to keep the sound that loud."

Robert felt like the chemistry building between them had unintentionally slipped away.

Perhaps it was just self-judgment over his hesitation. Feeling disorientated, he responded, "Yeah, that's pretty ridiculous."

They stood for several minutes in silence. Robert looked at the others in the line.

Everyone wore an expression of the wearied and harassed, a result of too much walking and the suspicion that they were being tricked into spending money. As the line advanced, he slowly moved forward with the herd, Molly matching his stride beside him. He was now close enough to see into the main staging area. Four foot tall metal dividers separated the guests, leading to what appeared to be an oversized silver RV. Inserts lay over the windows, making them appear like solid metal. As the rectangular vehicle began to vibrate, a thin glass partition came down from above. As soon as it concealed the ride, smoke filled the space between the double-paneled partition, creating a glowing white light over where the vehicle once stood.

Thinking that it was clever to build the ride in a drivable vehicle, Robert saw the alien barker high above on some type of platform, looking down on the queuing area, her white leotard the only color in the sea of black drapes surrounding her. Staring at her triggered him to look backward. The aisle directly behind him was still empty.

Assuming that perhaps this was the last shift and the crew running the place had closed the line, he turned to Molly. "Looks like this is a simulator ride. It's not too big, which at least explains why the line is moving so slowly."

"You can see all the way in there?" She stood on her toes, grabbing his shoulder for balance. It did nothing to help the view of the five-foot-two woman.

"Yeah, I can't see how many people are still ahead of us, though."

"That's all right. I'm enjoying the wait."

"I am, too." He wanted so much to say something romantic or even somewhat clever, but the awkwardness that he'd been out-running was catching up, as he'd known it eventually would. He forced a smile, gazing at the woman whom he wanted to accept his growing affection.

Silently, they stood in the tight bend of the hallway, listening to the mechanical whirl of the machinery simulating the space launch. When the last pneumatic sound was complete, there was a hiss, and the long glass panel disappeared into the darkness of the ceiling.

Seconds later, two automatic doors opened outward. With the group in front of him, he could only see heads coming off the ship. Oddly, everyone disembarking was male. Minutes later, the line shuffled forward again.

Once around the curve, the entire staging area came into view. The metal dividers separated the groups to align with the door openings. Signs reading *Men and Women* led up to the makeshift gates in large bold lettering with arrows pointing in opposite directions. The people in line obeyed the command and walked along in separate groups. The first to protest was the overweight man who'd laughed at Molly's comments earlier.

Robert strained to hear the argument. A taller woman dressed the same as the barker who'd originally lured Robert into the line was politely explaining that he would not be allowed to board with his companion. She added that it was an absolute requirement of the program and smiled, the movement extremely creepy in conjunction with her oval bug eyes. He put up a fuss until an extraordinarily tall man dressed in all black with oversized sunglasses approached them.

Robert was unsure what the overweight man said next, but assumed it was a demand for a refund. The tall man, moving gracefully for someone of his stature, pointed to a hallway at the back of the room. The man held the hand of the woman he was with and followed the man in black to what Robert figured was the exit.

He looked at Molly. "It looks like we're not allowed to ride together."

"Hey, if you don't want to ride with me, it's okay. I won't be offended."

"No, not at all! Up ahead, they're separating men and women before you get on the ride."

"Huh, that's effing weird, dude."

"Yeah."

"Why in the heck would they do that?"

They were only steps away from the separation point. "Don't know. Maybe weight distribution?" He didn't believe it, but it was the first thing that came to mind.

"What do you think? Do you still want to get on?"

"Dunno."

"Well... we did wait a long-ass time."

"Yeah, I guess."

The long-haired guy moved to the right. Robert's turn was next.

Molly leaned over and kissed Robert on the cheek. She rubbed away the lipstick smear and sweetly said, "That's for keeping me company and just in case the space mission doesn't make it." She snorted a laugh and moved to the left, joining the other women.

Robert wanted to grab her hand and walk out. It wasn't a hasty impulse; it was more like an instinct. Something suddenly felt very off about the entire room. Unable to act on the feeling, he watched Molly walk up and board the simulator vehicle. Standing among the group of men, he watched the doors close, and the vehicle began to vibrate slightly, shaking the reflective silver surface.

Suddenly, the booming noise filled the room once again. This time, it was nearly deafening. Seconds later, as the glass partition once again went down, he heard a ringing in his ears that seemed to penetrate all the way to his fillings, leaving them hurting.

Feeling queasy, Robert waited for the simulation to end. He checked his phone. It said six o'clock. Pissed that a phone that had cost nearly two weeks' salary couldn't even keep time, he peeked at the wristwatch of a guy wearing a *Twilight Zone* T-shirt. The time-piece was the old- fashioned kind that had Roman numerals and hands—the time matched his phone. Bewildered, Robert glanced around the space, his mind racing, trying to explain what could be happening.

The noise of the machine ebbed, and the heat it gave off dissipated. Robert looked up and saw the alien barker staring into an oversized tablet. Her hand moved so quickly across the screen that it appeared blurry. Assuming it was some trick of the light, he watched the smoke evaporate from the glass partition, and then the panel raised back up. The pneumatic sound was followed by the opening of the doors. One by one, the group of frowning women quickly stepped down to the ground. Robert watched as they carefully headed to the exit.

A voice came over the hidden loudspeaker. "And now, gentle-man, it's your turn to ride to our planet!"

Robert searched the room. Molly had not yet left the ride. Apprehensively, he followed the other men into the souped-up RV, expecting her to hop off at any second. Going up two stairs, puck lights shone on what looked like theater seats, and all pointed toward a large screen inside the vessel. The rectangular area was no larger than an extended cargo van. There were no other doors.

Watching the group go to their seats, Robert stepped back to the queuing area, not finding her. He looked up to the balcony where he'd just seen the alien woman and shouted, "Hey, I didn't see my friend come off the ride!" There was only silence. Louder, he shouted, "Hey, is anyone there?"

From inside the ride, a gruff voice yelled back, "Hey, buddy, why don't you hop in so we can get this thing going?"

"Hey, my—" Robert almost shouted "girlfriend." Instead, he said, "—friend disappeared!"

"Buddy, sorry your girl gave you the slip, but come on. Have a heart. You're holding up the whole show."

Robert tried to find someone, anyone, who was in charge. Finally, the tall man in black came out from the hallway.

"Sir, can you please enter the spacecraft so the other visitors can take their journey?"

The worker's dedication to the illusion of this being an alien spacecraft brought a wave of heat. "Screw your stupid ride. Where's my friend?"

"Sir, please calm down." The man in black took off his sunglasses.

Robert was astounded. The man was just a teenager, appearing 18 years old, tops. Feeling guilty for yelling at him, he said, "Is there a back door to the ride?"

"No, why?"

"Because the girl I came in here with did not come out."

There were loud obscenities coming from the interior of the spaceship now.

"Then you must have missed her getting off. There is no back door." The kid seemed scared as he looked toward the RV, hearing the angry patrons. "Can you please just get on the ride? It's less than ten minutes, then we can talk."

"I don't give a shit about the ride! Let them go."

Slouching his shoulders, the gawky teenager shouted up to the balcony. "Hey, Rachael, let her rip."

The alien barker above them gave a thumbs-up. Seconds later, the almost familiar sounds and vibrations began again.

"Who's in charge of this place?"

"Me, at least for this afternoon. This is my uncle's show, but he isn't here right now." The kid flinched as the sonic boom went off.

"Do you have any security cameras in here?"

"No."

"Great." He looked over the cloth-draped walls, wondering if she could be playing a joke.

Since that wasn't a realistic possibility, he asked, "Where the hell could she be?"

"Sir, I have no idea. Why are you so sure she didn't get off the ride?"

"How could she have done that without me seeing her? It's a single file line, and there's only one door." Robert pointed to the low railings that were used to herd the patrons in, emphasizing his point.

"Yeah, I guess you're right. Are you sure you saw her get on?"

"Yes." Doubt crept in, rearranging his memory. He'd been sure that he watched her get on, but now felt less certain. Growing frantic, the teenager's blank stare wasn't helping.

As he felt the vibration of the ride behind him, Rachael, the alien, entered the room. With her well-manicured nails, she fished beneath the outline of the bug lenses. With a gentle flick, she popped them off, revealing her own brilliant eyes surrounded by the faintest outline of spray adhesive. "What's the issue, Tom?"

"This man says his friend disappeared into the RV—uh, sorry, spaceship."

Robert saw the knowing smile flash between them. He was nearly ready to belt him when the room lit up with the lighting effect. He raised his hand, shielding his face.

Looking away, Rachael scurried out of the room, and Tom put his glasses back on.

Desperation crept up his chest, gripping him. Swallowing hard, he said, "Why do you separate the men from the women?"

"It was something my uncle thought up. He said it builds tension and makes the experience feel more authentic." With a solemn expression, he added, "Sorry if your girl ditched you, man."

Robert could see Rachael returning to her post on the upstairs balcony. "She didn't ditch me!"

Suddenly, the thought occurred to him that maybe one of the other women from the ride might have seen something. Looking at Tom, he nearly yelled, "I'll be right back."

Briskly, he jogged out of the RV queuing area and into the hallway, hoping that he could find some clue. He came out of the darkened area next to the restrooms. There was a constant ringing now, and he wondered if the sonic boom had possibly damaged his hearing. His eyes scanned the long hallway. There was now no noise coming from Concourse A.

No one was around. Passing the entrance to the washrooms, he entered the cavernous area. The main globe lights above the convention center revealed that half the vendors were gone. He watched the few who remained piling their merchandise into boxes of various shapes and sizes.

Immediately, he looked up at the clock mounted above the concession stand. It was exactly eight o'clock.

Robert ran to the first vendor table that still had an occupant, a white-haired man wearing a tweed blazer with patches at the elbows. The sign above the boxed comics read, "The Stars Our Destination," followed by "Fine Comics and Collectibles."

"Sir, what time is it?" Robert asked.

The dignified-looking man pulled back his sleeve. "Minute past eight. You all right? You don't look so hot."

"Frankly, no." Seeing a rent-a-cop in an ill-fitting uniform in the next aisle, Robert said thank you over his shoulder and dashed to the man whom he hoped could shed some light on whatever was happening.

After a frantic explanation, Robert, the white-haired comic vendor, and the security agent were snaking through the velvet ropes of the waiting area of the Alien Experience. When they made it to the queuing area, it was empty.

Robert ran to the fabric walls and pulled aside the black drapes, finding a drywall and bricks behind them. There were two hallways, the entrance, and the exit. There was no rolling garage door that the RV could have driven out of. He looked around for something—anything— that could confirm his sanity.

"What did you say the ride was called?" the security office asked.

Robert mouthed, "Alien Experience." He was running through what was becoming obvious: the ride did not exist.

The old man said what Robert was already thinking. "Are you sure you didn't just nod off?"

Robert looked at the questioning eyes of the security officer and the sympathetic expression of the comic book vendor. He slowly backed away from them, feeling foolish and insignificant.

"I'm sorry to waste your time." Ignoring their protests, he ran down the exit corridor and through Concourse A, past the few remaining vendors and the depression that hung in the air of the nearly vacant space that just hours ago had been filled with frenetic energy.

Two weeks later, Robert was in Ohio. He had just left the concierge table after picking up his three-day VIP for Collectecon. His Internet searches had yielded no results for the Alien Encounter other than many out-of-print paperbacks and an interesting-looking graphic novel. It was foolish to be here. He could neither afford the expense nor the time off from his job, yet he couldn't stay away.

Whether it made sense to be there or not, he was determined to settle his mind once and for all. He owed his sanity that much. In a mob of oddly dressed conventioneers, he went through the main gate, holding his entrance badge high enough for the muscular attendant to see. The space was much the same as the one he'd attended back in Chicago, with most of the same vendors. In his hotel room that morning, he'd studied the layout. There was no Alien Experience attraction, nor anything like it. When he got to the back wall of the main room, he saw the small entrance to the hallway.

Robert took a deep breath and walked behind two guys who looked twice his age; they were wearing proton packs and matching gray costumes. They turned right toward the entrance of the cafeteria, leaving Robert to enter the hallway alone. A few steps in, he saw the sign with the silver spaceship and the bug-eyed alien advertising the Alien Encounter. He took out his phone and took several pictures. Not a single image appeared on his screen.

Testing his camera, he took a picture of his backpack. The image was there. Thinking of Molly, he ignored the panic and continued into the dark corridor. With each step, he waited for the alien barker to pop out of the wall and confess to some form of a ridiculous practical joke.

When he turned the corner and was standing directly behind the tall man with a jean jacket and long hair, he no longer felt anything remotely comical about the situation. Pulling out his phone, ready to videotape the line, he noticed that an hour had passed since he entered the convention. Sweat coated his face. Moments later, there was a thunderous boom throughout the enclosed space. Robert flinched and spun around. Standing behind him was Molly in her hooded red T-shirt and leggings. She was holding her ears with the same brilliant, beautiful smile.

Robert leaned forward to hug the woman who had invaded his every thought ever since they'd first met. Quickly removing her hand from her ear, she planted it squarely on his chest.

"Woah, slow down there, buster! I know I'm hotter than S but come on."

Taken aback, he opened his mouth to speak. Fear flashed across her face. Shaking her head, she placed her index finger over her lips as her eyes darted to the corners of the room. Bewildered, he took a slight step back.

She forced a smile. "What the crap was that?" The words were strained, spoken in a nearly cracking voice.

"Molly, what's happening?"

"That noise? What the crap was that?" She peered around Robert, pointing with her chin. He turned to see what she was looking at. The long-haired guy had just turned the corner, leaving the corridor empty. There was a tug at Robert's shoulder. Molly, on her toes, flung her arms around him. Despite the confusion, her warm body pressing against his made him feel whole. It was the first time in his life that he'd ever felt anything like that. As he pulled her closer, he thought of the eye of a hurricane and tried to think of a way out.

Her breath tickled his ear as she whispered, "I knew you would come back. I knew you felt it too." She squeezed harder. "We mustn't let the others in line hear us."

Muffled by her hair, Robert said, "What's happening?"

"This place is stuck between time and space. I've been trapped here for longer than I can remember. In all this time, all I know for sure is that if the others catch on that they are trapped, they will make it impossible for either of us to leave."

"What?"

She clutched both of his hands. "I know this is insane, but please play along."

Robert pulled away. "I don't understand."

"Whether you do or not, our lives depend on what you choose to do next. If you go back the way you came, you will be stuck in an endless tunnel alone. If you move forward and play along, we have a chance. You're the first new person I've seen in a long time, but I've seen a few others make it out like you did."

"You're really freaking me out."

"Hey, pay attention!" She nudged him forward with a nod.

When Robert spun around, he saw the long-haired man peeking around the darkened corner. He had neither a nose nor a mouth, just piercing eyes. Molly pushed behind with both hands into Robert's back. He took a tentative step forward, his heart thudding.

In a whisper, he said, "That man had no mouth."

"That happens to most of us when there is no need to talk. I was like him until you showed up."

"*What*? How? Where are we?"

Faintly from behind, he heard Molly's pleading voice. "I wish I knew. All we can hope is that this is our turn."

"Turn for *what*?"

"Our chance to leave. Please, we must catch up with everyone."

"Molly, this is insane. Please, let's just go." He stared back at the direction he'd just come from; it was so dark that he couldn't see a sliver of light from the hallway. The realization that he also couldn't hear any sound reminded him of a documentary he had once watched about a black hole.

In a daze, he slowly stepped forward, rounding the dark corner to the lined room with four rows of people corded off by velvet ropes. It was the same group he'd seen in Chicago, except for the overweight man and his companion. With extra attention, Robert noticed that a few of the heads were missing ears, and the woman at the front of the line had no nose.

Desperately, he wanted to leave, to just run, and never look back, but when he glanced at Molly and saw her wide eyes, he simply could not. Whatever he'd stepped into, he could not leave her regardless of his fear, not after the torture of the last two weeks thinking he'd lost her forever.

"What is this, anyway? I couldn't get anything out of the alien Barbie doll with the big eyes. She is totally method with her demeanor and line delivery."

The cadence of her voice reminded him of an actress in a lame commercial. Robert stared at her, wanting her to stop the performance. She opened her eyes wide, miming for him to play along. He could feel the other conventioneers' eyes on him. In a slow, drawn-out voice, he played out his part like an actor in a mad play. "I'm really not sure... some type... of flight simulator, I think, maybe?"

"So, you're like me. You thought the sign looked cool and figured, what the hay." She put her hand forward, her fingers hanging down. "My name is Molly. Nice to meet you."

In his periphery, he could see the others slowly directing their attention forward, away from their now private show. He grabbed her hand, his stomach rumbling. "Robert."

Molly slid up next to him. "Not cutting, just figured it would be easier to talk this way... That is, if you want to. I don't want to be like one of those super annoying, unaware people on a plane that starts blabbing when everyone else is just like shut the eff up, man!"

Robert strained to remember his response. As he was about to say, "I like talking," a boom thundered throughout the room. Molly leaned forward, and even through the noise, he heard her.

"We cannot let the others know. We need to relive everything exactly. To them, this is their first time through. If they catch on now, they will never let us leave."

As the last echoes of the sound dissipated, Robert looked at his phone. Over two hours had gone by. He glanced behind Molly down the increasingly long corridor and saw the shapely silhouette of the alien barker in the shadow, emerging from the blackness that was slowly progressing toward him.

Taking a step backward, Molly grabbed and pulled at his sleeve, willing him into place.

She gave him a practiced smile. "Hey, pay attention."

Robert slowly turned around and closed the growing gap to the long-haired man, hoping he wouldn't turn around again and expose the patch of skin where his mouth should be. Looking into the main queuing area, the glass partition was now lower to the floor, filling with smoke.

As the next, much quieter boom reverberated in the tiny space, Molly whispered, "Thank you for coming back to me."

Robert thought to say, *I've never felt this way about another person*, but froze. The line advanced once again, the group moving too quickly, like a sped-up recording as they filled in the empty spaces before them. Robert, not knowing his place, went along complacently, feeling the seconds speed by. Everything was moving at a different pace. It was like venturing into a video game where time had no real value yet dictated space. With only four more couples to go before he and Molly got to the *Men and Women* signs, a couple he hadn't previously noticed began complaining to the taller alien girl.

The same as in Chicago, the tall man in glasses came out and took them away after a short conversation. With a sigh, a small tear trickled down Molly's face. Quickly, she wiped it onto her sleeve and smiled once again, the desperation in her eyes betraying her upturned colored lips.

Confused, Robert moved to the turnstile, expecting her to go first like the last time.

Standing beneath the *Men* sign, Molly leaned in and gave him a kiss on his cheek. "We're meant to be together, Robert. If I make it out this time, I will come back for you. I will do this as many times as I have to until we find a way out."

Robert numbly played his part, ambling along. Over the staticky loudspeaker, the male barker's voice came on. "Gentlemen, it's now your time to depart to our world."

Robert, not knowing what else to do, moved with the herd onto the RV. Apprehensively, he took one of the front seats nearest to the screen. As the compartment filled, he looked to the queuing area. As the doors slowly closed, he saw Molly standing among the other women as the darkness slowly gained on them, its shadows diminishing their features. The puck lights above went out, and the film began.

Within a minute, a psychedelic stream of colors emulated a spaceship speeding across the cosmos. A slight rocking and vibration accompanied the effects with classical music from a single monotone speaker, dulling the interlude.

Robert felt a sharp pain in his temple as his mind filled with thoughts that were not his own. He knew that this dark place at the edges of the convention was formed from his desire. On that lonely day at the convention, when his thoughts had conjured Molly as he entered the dark hallway, all the others in the line came with her, enhancing the illusion. Like a base instinct, he now deeply understood that he could end their existence, as well as Molly's, by doing something as simple as letting them in on his dream that was becoming real.

Knowing that Molly would also cease to exist if he freed himself right now, his heart nearly stopped beating. His face was now quickly tightening as the RV slowly disappeared into the vast darkness surrounding him, swallowing up the ceiling and walls. When the growing void finally reached him, he was back in line behind the long-haired man.

Robert didn't dare bring his hand to where his lips should be. To him, thinking and knowing were two very different things. In a place where time did not exist, he stood frozen in frustrated silence, wishing for Molly's return. He fought the growing claustrophobic angst over the next two weeks with the knowledge that, soon, it might be their turn to live the life they were meant to live.

HOME AGAIN

Matt, thinking of his dead friend, sat idling in the parking lot, waiting for his wife and nephews to finish their costume shopping at Riley's Trick Shop. It had been years since he'd been back in New Bremen, and not much had changed. The storefronts were nearly the same, except for the few that were now vacant. He was staring at the ice cream shop his mother used to take him to whenever he got an A in school. Nostalgia for a time and place he struggled to forget was getting to him.

Wondering how long the shops had been closed, he began rolling up his window, wishing he could stop intrusive thoughts as simply as he could shield himself from the breeze. Hovering clouds were competing with the very late fall sun, taking its warmth, possibly for the last time of the year. Just before the window shut out the cool air, he heard faint music that brought his attention to the sidewalk.

Matt flinched when he saw what couldn't be. Standing in front of Big Bear Sports and Archery with "My Sharona" blaring through a Walkman, a nearly forgotten teenage face with his headband and matching Adidas sweatshirt got off his golden ten-speed. The song, the bike, and the memory of his friend flooded his senses with images of drinking from hoses, swimming in over-chlorinated pools, and biking all day until the streetlights came on.

The music faded as the rider entered the sporting goods store. Turning off the engine, Matt walked trance-like to the bike that, throughout his childhood, had grown into legend as an unbeatable machine, regardless of the opponent. More than any girlfriend, it was the neighborhood's most equally envied and hated possession. Staring through the heavily decaled window of the store, he watched the rider walk past the counter. He moved with an odd fluidity that made the tall, wiry kid seem graceful, just as Matt had remembered him.

Glancing back at Riley's, Matt walked up the cracked concrete steps to the entrance of the outdated sporting goods store. Mr. Luger, the store's owner, stood behind the counter, surrounded by the many taxidermy specimens he had accumulated over the years. They were a mixture of the beautiful and the bizarre. The most notable was a quail, posed midflight, inside an alligator's jaws.

Not only did the proprietor look identical to the way he had during Matt's last visit some 30 years ago, but the merchandise displays hadn't seemed to change either. Everything was painted in the earth-tone colors that had been popular in the early '80s. Even through the glass, he could smell decay and rotten water from the fish tanks lining the back wall, which were filled with a mixture of exotic baits and other aquatic oddities.

Ignoring everything else, Matt looked down the back aisle to the glass-door refrigerators.

Standing in front of them was a teenager who was the spitting image of Joey K, with his black sponge earphones dangling around his neck. The gangly teen was fishing through a Styrofoam cup, most likely looking for the one with the most nightcrawlers, the way his friend always used to. Matt would have sworn it had to be Joey's son, but reminded himself that dead teenagers don't have offspring.

Bewildered, Matt equally wanted to laugh and cry, staring at what life had taught him had been his only true friend, whose life had been extinguished before the age of 19. Since grammar school, Joey had looked past Matt's many flaws and seemingly endless neuroses and introduced him to a world that all the other boys in the neighborhood had taken for granted. A world where every day was spent together searching out a new adventure, bringing a closeness between two friends that everyone else shunned.

Shifting in the glass's reflection, Matt saw his former teenage self with his long, curly hair and sporadic acne. His clothes had also changed. He was now wearing a wrinkled *Return of the Jedi* T-shirt and camouflage pants. Pulling at the thin fabric, his finger got snagged in the hole that had been put there from a BB gun fight.

Matt's iPhone vibrated in his pocket, startling him so much that he nearly fell off the front step of the store. He felt that if he brought modern technology into what he was witnessing, both would cease to exist. Although he was completely alone, the words from so long ago echoed in his head, as if the sound came from a loudspeaker:

"Are you coming with, or what?"

The words felt heavy, as if they were weighing Matt down and making his knees weak. It was the last thing Joey had ever said to him at the end of a terrible argument, resulting in his friend riding alone that night and never returning.

Nobody knew how Joey had ended up in the lake. All they knew was that when they'd found him floating on the shore a week later, there had been no signs of trauma other than the bruises his lifeless body had sustained from banging against the rocks. That had extinguished their grand plan to ride off to endless summers, drifting south to the warmth and avoiding adulthood and all its constraints for as long as possible. The guilt over letting his friend go alone had never left.

Pulling himself from his tragic memories, he saw in the reflection his wife, Cassie, with their nephews, standing in front of the car and looking up and down the street. His own image was that of a middle-aged man once again.

Glancing into the store, he saw Mr. Luger, now with gray hair and liver-spotted hands, throwing some eagle-claw hooks into a paper bag for his customer. The man was the only patron in the store.

Matt walked carefully back to the car, wondering if guilt and lack of sleep could cause hallucinations. To his wife, he said, "Sorry, I, ah, kind of wandered off." He wanted to tell her what he'd just experienced, but instinct kept the words inside.

His partner squinted, tilting her head to the side to examine him. "Are you okay?"

Shaking away the memories, he grunted, "Yeah." Not wanting to worry her, he bent down to one knee and checked out the costumes that the eager boys thrust at him. After a morning-long fight, they both agreed to be Thor, but one with a hammer and the other with a shield. After mindlessly voicing his approval, he peered over the heads of his sister's children at the sporting goods store. The bike that had drawn him in was gone.

Cassie came up close, whispering, "Seriously, are you all right? You're white as a gh—"

"*Yes.*" He felt bad for cutting her off, but that was the last word he needed to hear or contemplate right now. "I didn't get much sleep and could use a beer and a sandwich."

She smiled, which she perfected over the years, the one that said, *All right, I'll let you get away with the lie as long as you snap out of your funk.* She massaged his arm. "Well, that's easy enough to accommodate." Placing her hand on top of the boys' heads, she said, "Okay, avengers, let's get loaded into your chariot."

Matt looked back at the store. Images of biking, Joey, and the town ran through his mind.

Reason was trying to convince him that maybe he had dozed off and dreamt it all. Getting into the rental, his inner voice echoed,

You'd better take a hard turn before you get too far down memory lane.

It was Friday night, and after getting his temporary wards to sleep, Matt sat on the swinging bench on the front porch of his mother's house. The last two years since his father had passed were not kind to her. First, her hip went, then her memory. A sense of duty mixed with guilt for leaving all the responsibility to his sister brought him back.

He had enough beer that, although still anxious, Matt had the sense he could make it through another few days. Swaying there and doing his best to let his thoughts drift, he remembered all the meals he'd enjoyed while sitting between his parents in the same spot. Wishing he could just once feel that safe again, he grabbed his phone and called his sister for the nightly check-in.

"So, have my monsters devoured you yet?"

"Close, but not quite."

"Really, though, how are they... and Mom?"

The worry in her voice hurt. He knew he wasn't her first choice to fill in. "All is good. I got them down without too much effort. Mom has been a little off, but they're all asleep right now, and I'm on the front porch, getting ready to open another beer."

"Lucky you."

Yeah, stuck in the suburbs, thinking of a dead friend. What else could I ask for? "How's the training going?"

"Boring but necessary, or at least someone thinks it is. How's Cassie holding up? I know she isn't exactly the domestic type."

"That's mean. Correct... but mean." He let out a laugh. "She's fine playing the part of Super Aunt as long as it's for a short time. She just ran out to BMart to stock up on candy for tomorrow."

Matt could see a bike approaching at the end of the street. Its front light flickered through the darkness, and music was playing.

He thought he recognized the phantom lyrics of "My Sharona" wafting through the air.

"She didn't have to do that. I told her there was plenty of candy in the pantry."

He barely heard her as the bike went under a streetlamp, confirming his fear. Anxiety crept up his arms, cooling his skin. The bike was picking up speed and heading toward the house. It was moving much too fast, and the rider was way too stiff, almost as if they were glued in place.

Distracted, he responded, "Yeah, but you know her... she's a people pleaser."

As the bike approached the driveway, it came to a near stop. Matt couldn't make out much more than a vague shape on the golden ten-speed. It conjured memories of being frightened of the dark, bringing the urge to run and hide. Wondering what could possibly be happening, he sat frozen as the rider waved slowly, disappearing into the darkness.

Seeing ghosts again, Matt?

He shook his head, knowing he had to stop the morbid thoughts that had clung to him since he'd arrived back in town. His sister's voice distracted him from the panic.

"You sound down."

Stop overreacting. It's just a kid on a bike. It took effort to say, "Lots of memories coming at me." He added, "I don't know how you still live here."

"Well, one of us had to stay behind."

Anger flashed. *Well, one of us had to get a real job and pay for our parents' care.*

Squeezing the beer, he let the thought go. The last thing he needed right now was to get dragged into a fight; neither would ever win and would only stretch his nerves further. "Yeah, I suppose so."

"Anyway, it's not so bad being around people you know. After a while, you kind of always know what to expect. It takes time, but you find genuine comfort in routine."

Changing the subject before the conversation turned into a lecture, he said, "So, any specifics for the boys tomorrow?"

"Nope, it's the one day I don't limit their sugar." In a hurried voice, she added, "Within reason, of course!"

Yeah, I'm so irresponsible I would let them do whatever they want. "Sounds good. Hey, I hate to cut you short, but I think I heard Ma." The lie felt way too natural.

"All right. Thanks again for all your help."

"Of course." Leaning back and looking down the street that used to be his path to freedom, he sat and drank, thinking of the sports store.

He had come up with a dozen excuses for what he thought he'd seen, but deep in his gut, where it mattered, he thought he knew the truth. Somehow, his friend had given him a glimpse of a different place and time. As the beer made its way to his head, he rocked slowly, trying to forget the day.

The next afternoon, the sidewalks were filled with ghosts, witches, and goblins, kicking up fallen leaves as they raced up lawns, hoping to add to their already overflowing bags of candy. Matt was fighting to keep up with the enthusiastic boys.

As they approached Currant Street, he wanted to turn away, but reluctantly followed as they made their way up to Mrs. K's door. As they fought about who was going to ring the bell, the door popped open. Like everything else in town, Joey's mother was recognizable, but weathered.

Smiling, she said, "Matty! It is so nice to see you." She took a step down, weaving past his nephews, and hugged him. As she pulled away, he noticed she smelled of the same perfume and hint of garlic as always. The woman who seemed to live in her kitchen gripped his arm and said in her squeaky voice, "It has been much too long. Please come in."

Attempting to pull away, he said, "I'd love to, but I have the boys."

"*Oh*, they can stop for a minute." Looking down at the four- and eight-year-olds, she added, "Come along, boys, and I will give you Rice Krispies Treats." Her brilliant white dentures were stained with lipstick as she smiled. "There are M&M's on top!"

The boys dashed through the door, knocking into one another, with their plastic bags dangling behind them. Matt followed, entering a hallway he remembered being much larger. Mrs. K gripped his arm tightly as if she could sense his reluctance to enter the house where he'd spent so much time when growing up.

When they got to the kitchen, it was like staring into a time capsule. The appliances were olive green, and the Formica counter had metal surrounding the edges.

She yelled upstairs, "Joe, come on down. Matty is here!"

He finally pulled completely free without being aggressive. Although she was summoning her husband, the image of Joey coming down the stairs danced through his mind.

Swiping a casserole dish off the counter, she bent down. "Here, boys, take your treats." She handed them each a cellophane-wrapped snack the size of a bar of soap. As they fought to tear them open, she said to Matt, "Susie told me you were filling in this week. I'm so glad you stopped by."

It was senseless and childish, but Matt wanted her to instantly stop using their childhood names. Each time he heard it, it was like a violation, making every nerve taut. Hiding the misplaced annoyance, he said, "I am too."

"I don't remember the last time I saw you. It has to have been several years."

He wanted to remind her that he made it a point to call every year around the holidays, but politely replied, "It certainly has been a while."

"How's your mom?"

Her look let him know she was aware, but wanted to hear it from him. The small-town gossip knew everything. "Honestly, not well."

"I'm so sorry to hear that." She placed the casserole dish back on the counter and wiped her hands on her apron. "I saw Susie last week at the grocery store. She was beside herself with happiness that you were coming in to help. The poor girl has so much on her plate with your mom and the boys."

The room felt as if the heat went up 10 degrees. Hundreds of aromas from past meals were assaulting his nostrils, making them itch. "Yeah, I know. I try to make it out here as much as possible, but my work doesn't afford me much free time."

"I understand."

She gave him the sideways look she used to give when she caught them swearing. It was a mixture of understanding and forced shame. Feeling like a child again, he looked away, the urge to leave growing. The boys were inhaling the treats so quickly that the plastic wrap was dangerously close to being devoured.

"Nephews, watch the plastic, all right?"

They nodded in unison, shoving the gooey mess farther down.

Figuring after some quick small talk that he could use the boys as an excuse to leave, he said, "So, how have you been?"

Her eyes flashed, showing the pain of the last few years. "Keeping busy. Mr. K retired, so we are now living out our golden years."

"Good for him."

Abruptly changing the subject, she said quietly, "You know it will be thirty years this Sunday."

He was amazed she had held out this long without bringing up the death that she still blamed Matt for. "Yes, I remember."

"Not a day goes by that I don't." She took a quick step forward, grasping his forearm. "What was he doing out on that road that night, Matty?"

They'd had this conversation after the accident so many times he wanted to scream. "Mrs. K, I would prefer not to talk about this in front of the boys."

"It's just a question. There's no harm in that!" Her face became flushed, her forehead now matching the rouge on her cheeks. In a disgusted voice, she screamed upstairs, "Joe, where are ya!"

"He doesn't have to come down, really." Knowing she was already upset, he asked the question that could stop the nonsensical thoughts that had been echoing in his mind since the day before. "Do you still have Joey's old bike?"

Her head leaned far back, as if a gust of wind had struck her. "Of course. It's in the garage in the same place we put it the night the police brought it back."

His stomach rolled over. "Do you mind if I take a look at it?" Her eyes became narrow slits. "Suit yourself."

Finally, she gave a knowing smile that felt almost sexual from the desire in her gaze.

Disgusted, he walked to the front hallway and opened the door leading to the garage.

As the door opened, the smell of oil was overwhelming. Taking the single step down, his entire body flinched as he peered through the dark space, seeing the shadow in the shape of a person. Logic was trying to beat out the fear as he stared at what appeared to be someone sitting on the bike. Disorientated, he realized he was looking at an oversized cutout of a photo of Joey grinning an almost cartoonish smile. The life-size cardboard cutout was positioned to make it look like Joey was riding.

A ragged Adidas sweatshirt covered the paper-thin teenager's torso. Mismatched shoes were duct-taped to the sweatpants' legs, and the hands looked like someone had twisted together oversized pipe cleaners around gardening claws to resemble fingers. Realizing this was a sort of deranged shrine to their dead son, Matt stumbled out of the garage and yanked the door shut. Just before it closed, the figure appeared to smile.

Matt slipped the top bolt in place. For a few seconds, he held the knob, expecting the paper-thin man to yank the door open. *Could that have been what you saw at the hardware store? Is she crazy enough to bring this thing outside?*

Taking a deep breath, he stepped backward into the kitchen. The room felt warmer.

Fighting the urge to confront the woman, who he now was thoroughly convinced was off her rocker, he blurted out, "We really have to get going."

He grabbed Rick and Todd by the shoulders and yanked them forward. "Okay, guys, let's go get some more candy."

Are you coming, or what?

His heart thudded in his chest. What he thought was his dead friend's voice made him look at the closed door, expecting to see the paper Joey walking toward him.

"Ah, please, can't you stay? Just a few more minutes. I have to talk to you, Matty."

She took a step toward him. He spun, freeing his sleeve from her grip. As her fingertips swiped the flannel, he felt that if she grabbed him, he would never be able to free himself from her again—that he would be stuck in limbo in this room that never changed, at her mercy, forced to continually answer her questions about her lost son.

Wanting to lash back at her for the growing fear, Matt almost blurted out that Joey had been on the road that night because he needed to be away from her and the abusive asshole upstairs. Fighting the urge, he ushered the boys down the hallway. Without looking back, he shoved his nephews out the front door.

As the night canceled the daylight, he followed the boys zombie-like as they ran door-to- door. Having hundreds of memories at once was disorienting. Each ended with the realization that his friend was no longer alive, making his mood match the darkening sky. No amount of love, longing, or sense of right and wrong was ever going to change that.

Walking along the fallen leaves, Matt desperately wanted to go back to his mother's house and Cassie to self-medicate the images away, but he couldn't take the enjoyment from the boys. Regardless of what had happened in his own youth, he couldn't let the past take away from their future.

It was almost fully dark as they approached the woods surrounding the lake. Matt wanted to avoid the area entirely, but it would add half a mile to their walk to avoid taking the bike path. It was now the only responsible choice with the cold front coming, as he'd forgotten the boys' jackets.

The children ran ahead, following the snaking path, already chattering about the goodies they would trade when they got home. Fueled by sugar, they charged forward, gaining more distance from their uncle despite his protests. As he watched them near the bend, a bike approached in the distance. With the moonlight flashing across the golden frame, Joey sped along, whistling a tune that sounded like a waltz.

Matt stood frozen in place. He couldn't fool himself that this was a hallucination or a stored memory. He knew his friend was back. His heart rate increased as he looked ahead. The boys were no longer in his line of sight. There was only the bike with a shadow on its seat. As it neared, it moved painfully slowly, the rider effortlessly staying balanced despite looking like he was at a standstill.

The familiar voice called out before the face was close enough to see clearly, "Are you coming with, or what?"

Matt wanted to run but stood stuck, barely able to catch his breath. Now, feet away, the rider completely stopped and walked the last few steps, guiding his bike at his side. In the near blackness, the face appeared to be only a thin photograph with moving lips. Matt's tears chilled his warm skin. They were not from fear—that was bottled away—but from his lost friend.

"You in, or what?"

"No." It was all he could utter.

The paper shadow fluttered as the wind howled past. "You know, the lake wanted us both that night, Matty."

The words felt like thoughts plucked from his mind. Something always told him he would pay for dodging fate so long ago. Like a kite fighting the wind, Joey came closer, wobbling, as his eyes glowed in the moonlight.

Matt stepped slowly backward. The gravel made it impossible to keep his balance. "Please, just leave me alone."

"Matty, are you coming, or what?"

All the guilt and doubt rose up again as he saw the claw that was Joey's hand glistening in the moonlight, waving him closer. The welcoming gesture from the makeshift hand made him nauseous. Despite his panic, he needed to know.

"Where've you been all this time?" The words were a whisper gobbled up by the chirping of insects.

"You're about to find out."

In a flash, the claw-like hand swung down, cracking Matt's skull.

***

Cassie sat on the porch, staring at her unanswered texts. Just as she was about to call Matt, their nephews appeared through the trees from the bike path. She stood, waving. They ran toward the house, pushing each other and giggling as they got closer to her, thoroughly investigating their loot. Curious, Cassie kept looking at the path.

As they climbed the stairs, she asked, "Where's your uncle?"

"I dunno. He was right behind us."

They dashed through the screened door, letting it slam. Cassie stayed on the porch, staring at the path and the glimmering lake beyond. She called twice, but both attempts went straight to voice-mail.

Walking down the stairs, she saw a teenager on a ten-speed fly out of the path. The gangly rider was dressed in an overstuffed sweatsuit with muffled music accompanying him.

Seconds later, following behind was a much shorter rider fighting to keep up. As the awkward teenager passed, Cassie thought he heard him scream out, "Please make it stop!"

Glancing his way, she saw a clever mask that appeared to be as thin as a sheet of paper. His eyes and nose vaguely reminded her of Matt. Ignoring whatever childish prank they were pulling, Cassie quickly walked to the front of the expansive path, calling for her husband. A week later, Matt's body was found washed up on shore.

BALZAR'S LAST ACT

"I won't hurt her if you cooperate."

His daughter's room was so dark that Mike could barely make out the silhouette of the intruder what he did see made him feel sick. Glaring at the glowing face hovering over Vivian, Mike knew he had to be still asleep, but his pounding heart brought doubt.

The edge of a wide butcher knife caught a streak of moonlight, illuminating his daughter's sleeping face. The impulse to leap forward and tackle the man who'd climbed in from the window made Mike shake. The knife was too close to her to take the gamble. Instead, he feebly asked, "What did you say?"

"I need you to do something for me." The crazy man's voice cracked on the last word as he laughed, sounding like he had gravel in his throat.

In the dim light, the shadow looked like an enormous clown face floating on top of a spindly body. "I don't have any real money here. Not more than maybe twenty bucks. Payday isn't until Friday," Mike said.

"I don't need your money. Your job is why I'm here."

Mike took a step closer, his eyes glued to the knife, imagining the blade piercing Vivian's skin. Sweat oozed out of every pore.

"My... job. What? Why? You must have me mistaken for someone else. I'm a janitor."

"Yes, who has keys to the museum. I need you to get something for me from the magician's exhibit."

Mike thought he was possibly dealing with an addict. The quick cadence of his voice, and his fidgety hands, reminded him of those burdened with addiction. Thinking he could possibly reason with the man who held his daughter's life in balance did little to calm him.

"Please. Just leave." He swallowed hard. "I won't call the cops. Just walk away, and it'll be like none of this happened." Mike stared at the beady eyes, trying to guess the intruder's thoughts.

Screeching laughter erupted from the stranger. With his free hand, he covered his enormous lips, which stretched ear-to-ear.

Mike glanced at Vivian's face. She stirred, but somehow remained asleep. The intruder took a small step back. Moonlight from the open window removed the shadow covering his face. What Mike was hoping was a trick of his imagination was confirmed by the dim light. The man holding the butcher knife was made up to look like a clown.

The pasty white makeup was interrupted by large, arching, and pencil-thin eyebrows and a red mouth so big that the lips looked like they would swallow up the face. A round nose was crookedly attached, like a partially deflated balloon.

"I caution you to ignore the laughter." The lispy voice was disrupted by another chuckle that was muffled by a gloved hand. The long fingers parted, exposing crooked, stained teeth. "If you don't cooperate, I will do whatever I must."

The knife came closer to Vivian, its pointy tip inches from her face. Tensing, Mike raised his hands in a halting motion. "Buddy, I'll do whatever you want. Please, please, get that away from her."

The clown's painted eyes opened wider, glistening in the moonlight. "This can be over quickly and without anyone getting hurt. I just need you to get into the museum and go to Exhibit

Eight. There, you will find a magician's bag. It's labeled Balzar's Bag of Tricks. Inside, there will be a jar of transforming powder."

"You want what? Powder? You're threatening my daughter for that? It can't be worth anything."

"It's everything."

Vivian turned, pulling on her worn Care Bears blanket Mike had gotten her at the thrift store.

"Look, I'll get you whatever you want, pal." He thought Vivian was still asleep. Despite his own fear, he was thankful for that. He couldn't cope with the thought of her waking up to a madman hovering over her. Trying to sound calm, he said, "We can go right now, okay?" He gestured toward the door, attempting to lure him out of the room.

"I can't go with you. You'll go and get it." He chewed on his lower lip, making the makeup around his lips wrinkle.

"Look, I'm not leaving her alone with you."

"You haven't a choice." With the tip of the knife, he caressed the blanket, edging closer to her tiny head. "Don't test me. Her life means nothing to me."

Mike clenched his fists. One flick of the clown's wrist could end life as he knew it.

Desperate, he pleaded, "Look, I'll give you the keys. You would have to hide from only a single security guard this early. You will be in and out."

"I can't go!"

There was no longer any doubt that the man was insane and could not be reasoned with. As Mike contemplated his next move, Vivian sat up, rubbing sleep from her eyes. "Daddy, why are you yelling?"

The urge to hug his four-year-old overwhelmed him. Trying to sound calm, he said, "Go back to sleep, Sugarplum." It was too late. Looking up, her mouth opened wide as she shrieked. The clown slapped his hand across her mouth, muffling her with a dirty-gloved hand.

Putting the knife just below her throat, he cried out, "Go now, and leave your phone!" He let out a sharp, piercing cackle. "If you call the police when you get there, you'll never see her again."

Mike's eyes were glued to the glistening metal against her soft skin, trying to will the man away with his stare. Witnessing Vivian losing a piece of her innocence at the hand of a demented clown brought waves of nausea. Desperate to take her pain away, he called out, "Please. Can't we come up with another plan?"

"Go, now!"

The madness in the man's eyes stopped any thought of rushing the deranged man. Mike knew deep inside that he had no choice. He had to leave, but he still stood frozen, unable to move. Taking a deep breath, he said, "Honey, Daddy has to go out for a few minutes."

Her muffled shriek of "no" ran through him like acid in his veins. Slick sweat covered his skin, trying to cool the burning furnace inside him. "It'll be all right, honey, I promise."

"Put your phone down, now."

Mike obeyed, placing it on Vivian's dresser. His stomach was beginning to spasm. "Viv, I'll be back soon. Everything will be all right."

Just as he was walking out of the room, imagining the clown harming his child, Mike vomited into his hand as he walked through the tiny kitchenette out the door.

Eight hours later, he sat slumped at his kitchen table, feeling as if whatever energy was normally stored inside a human being had been permanently removed. When he left his apartment, he'd run to the first floor, waking his landlord, and called the police. As he waited for them to come, he watched through the peephole for the man to go down the front stairs as his landlord watched the backfire escape.

Their efforts hadn't paid off. When the police arrived, they found his apartment empty.

They explained that the man possibly went to the roof and then to the adjoining building to escape. The female detective in charge had been the only one to reassure him that he'd made the right choice by calling them in. The other officers stared at him accusingly, adding to Mike's paranoia that his choice might have cost him his daughter. After an hour had gone by, no call had come, reinforcing his fear. Every minute that ticked by brought a growing emptiness like nothing he had ever experienced. This was even worse than when Vivian's mother abandoned them without so much as a text.

Searching for answers, he had spent the last hour scouring the Internet for any information on the bag the man was holding his daughter hostage for, hoping it would lead him back to Vivian. After endless searching, he finally found a website dedicated to stories of the unexplained. Desperately, he read:

Balzar the Great was a Hungarian-born magician who, in the early 1900s, had a reputation for being so gifted that many believed he had actually mastered the dark arts. His act was mainly what would be expected: sawing a woman in half, rabbits in hats, etc., but he had a specialty that, year after year, kept filling audiences in the playhouses he toured. The larger- than-life magician was known for having the ability to permanently change people's appearance.

Despite his popularity, the magician was rumored to be a volatile man who struggled with his temper. In several towns where he performed, Balzar reportedly had incidents with locals who were after his wife. Liska was ten years his junior, and many described her as the most alluring woman they had ever seen.

In the town of New Bremen, Illinois, where the magician's family had immigrated to when Balzar was a young man, an audience member by the name of Aikman was reported to have been turned into a ventriloquist's dummy as part of the act when the unsuspecting man made a pass at the magician's assistant. On stage, after a lotion was boiled into smoke, Aikman first looked wooden and, as the act progressed, appeared to shrink to the size of a small child. The stunned audience applauded as they watched the unbelievable illusion.

Later that evening, several townspeople reported a miniature wooden man walking up and down Main Street in the middle of the night, begging for help. Most suspected that the doll was a prop used to promote the show. However, Aikman's cousin claimed he'd spoken to the tiny man, and the dummy had intimate knowledge of their family. Days later, a missing person's report was filed, and Aikman was never heard from again.

Mike's blood felt like syrup sludging its way through his veins as he looked at a hand drawing of a doll-like man walking up a suburban street. It had a long ghostlike shadow and a look of terror on the fake face that made Mike's heart skip a beat. Scrolling past the terrible image, he went back to the article, holding his phone farther away, as if it would protect him from what he was absorbing.

Years later, just after Balzar came to another Midwestern town, a man showed up at a local hospital looking like a salamander. Doctors were baffled by the skin condition and sought to find the lotion Balzar had used in his act to see if an allergic reaction could have been the cause. Before anyone could locate the magician, the reptilian man passed away. During the autopsy, his internal organs were discovered to be human despite his outward appearance.

The rumors grew and spread that Balzar kept magical potions in a bag that was always at his side. They were reported to be able to conjure spirits and change the appearance of those who were unfortunate enough to come into contact with them. Just before he would perform, Balzar was known to lock himself away and meditate for days as he added ingredients to the potions and tonics.

When the potions were ready, as part of his act, Balzar would heat them up or rub them on select audience members, who would then act like farm animals, statues, or whatever else the audience would ask for. The performances were so convincing that most thought the participants chosen from the audience had been planted as part of the act.

In a time before the internet, the legend of the magician's skills spread by word of mouth.

Seeing him became a rite of passage for anyone who believed magic existed.

In the late 1970s, after disappearing for nearly ten years, Balzar gave his final performance, selling out the Chicago Visiting Star Theater. The link below is the only recorded footage of the once-famous magician. A local woman was called onto the stage, and after lotion was applied, she was made to look like a chicken. Pay particular attention to the stage floor.

Mike brought the phone close to his face, peering at the blurry video. The audio quality was so bad that he could hear nothing but buzzing static as he watched an attractive woman move like a chicken. After bobbing her head, her nose appeared to extend, and her eyes shrank to tiny dots. Clucking as feathers appeared on her bare arms, she squatted, and an egg appeared on the stage beneath her skirt. At that moment, the elderly magician stared directly into the camera, giving a look of such deep understanding that it should never grace a human's face. The piercing eyes reminded Mike of the clown he had seen in his child's room.

When his phone buzzed, Mike nearly jumped out of his skin. Seeing it was Detective Bradley, he clicked the answer button.

"Mr. Williams?"

"Yeah." His voice sounded like a frog croaking as he clicked out of the video. The image of the magician's eyes burned into his brain as he recalled the terror of watching the clown grab his daughter. "What's going on?" The desperation in his own voice brought a tear. As he wiped at it, he wondered how long someone could cry before they ran out of tears.

"We've found the man."

Adrenaline coursed through him as hope grew. "And Vivian?"

"Well, no. But we're bringing him to the station to interrogate him."

Her cry, like a phantom, echoed in his skull. *You should've just gotten the man his bag. The same way you should've gotten a real job and Vivian's mother would still be around.* The self-loathing was crushing him. "I'll be there in a few minutes."

"That would be good. I do need to caution you. Don't get your hopes up. He's not all there."

"What do you mean?"

"He's severely mentally disturbed."

Not wanting to hear the warning that his daughter could be gone forever, he whispered, "I'll be there as soon as I can."

He hung up. Sitting in the silence, images of the clown's face and the insane laughter echoed in Mike's mind. Leaning back in his chair, he stared out the window into the city. "Oh, baby, where are you?"

He pulled Vivian's blanket from his lap and breathed it in, smelling the cheap fruity shampoo they used. Tracing the edges of the cartoon bears that his daughter had come up with ridiculous names for, he whispered, "Please, please be all right." His voice cracked on the last word as he wept.

───────

Mike was sitting at the police station, drinking coffee as thick as motor oil. Every sip removed all the saliva from his mouth and throat. In the kinetic mess surrounding him, he stared at the door through which Detective Bradley had dragged the clown to question him.

The longer he sat, the more doubt grew, making him question every decision he had made in the last four years since Vivian was born. Why hadn't he worked harder? If he had, Balzar wouldn't have targeted them. Why didn't he rush the man instead of leaving an innocent child alone? As he struggled with these thoughts, and dozens of others, the room was growing warm, so warm he was coated with sweat.

Pulling him from his internal turmoil, Bradley came out of the interrogation room, looking years older than she had just a few hours ago. The oppressive fluorescent lighting made the bags under her eyes look like pillowcases. When she saw Mike, she made a pathetic attempt at a smile.

Mike stood and nearly sprinted to her, hoping for good news.

Bradley nodded toward a hallway to the right, with benches flanking its walls. It was littered with people who looked as if they had come from another planet. None of their clothes matched, and the expressions on their faces seemed cartoonish.

When he was close to Bradley, he asked, "Well, did you get him to talk?"

"Ah... yes." She smelled like the man—rotten in the way wet garbage always smelled.

"Where is she?"

"He won't say."

"Are you kidding me?" Mike grabbed her arm, halting her progress. Her look made him jerk it away instantly. "Sorry."

She carefully straightened her jacket. "It's okay. It's been an emotional few hours."

"How'd you get him to talk?"

Her keen stare made Mike feel nude. It was like she was hypnotizing him. "It's like I told you. He's mentally ill. I've worked him over, and he keeps insisting he's a magician named Balzar. I hate to say it, but traditional methods aren't going to work here, so we've called in a shrink."

The man's soulful eyes from the video floated through his head. *Balzar? No. How could it be?* His heart pounded furiously. "I don't know, or care, what this man's problem is. You need to get back in there and make him talk. Don't you understand? Vivian's out there alone!"

The outburst brought stares. A man who was missing a few fingers raised his hand in a Bronx cheer before he went back to staring at the ceiling, loudly counting the tiles.

"We're doing everything we can. This man's sick in a way I haven't seen before. I'm hoping the shrink can open him up." She shivered, rubbing her arms. "You know, on his face... well, that's not makeup. We tried washing it off. It must be some kind of a tattoo, or something.

Officer Schmidt, who watched him change, said his whole body was tattooed white, just like his face." Her eyes narrowed. "Weirder than that, his gloves appear to be sewn on... embedded into his skin. We will have to get a paramedic down here to see if they can cut them off, so we can print him. When we tried to remove them, he screamed like he was dying."

Picturing the thin man undressed, his stomach muscles tightened. "How long before the doctor gets here?"

"Shouldn't be more than fifteen minutes. Like I said before, it's important you don't get your hopes up. He's pretty far gone. When I asked him why he didn't go to the museum and steal the bag, he said his wife, Liska, was guarding it. He told me she's now a mannequin in the display. In a fit of rage, he changed her into a plastic woman when he found out she was cheating on him."

Mike remembered the beautiful form of a woman in the display that he passed every evening when he buffed the floors. Somehow, the story of a 120-year-old magician climbing through a bedroom window was becoming plausible, igniting the fear that was devouring him. He couldn't hear any more of this. "I need some air. Please call me if anything changes."

"I understand." She tucked her hair behind her ear. "We have people here if you need to talk to someone."

"Thanks." Unable to wait for information that might never come, Mike was determined to fetch the powder from the museum. He didn't know if it mattered anymore, but with every passing minute, he was growing surer that it was the only way to get his daughter back.

***

Before the sun rose, Mike entered the museum exhibit, which opened with a fake woman's legs hanging out of a small box and a wax figure of a magician with a cloak over his face, happily sawing away. With most of the lights off, the mannequins and magicians' tricks that were displayed held a menace he had never noticed before. After passing a large box with a moon on it, Mike stopped at the Balzar diorama.

At the back of the display was a mannequin of a woman surrounded by odd gadgets. She had wavy brown hair and was dressed in a skimpy outfit. Her glass eyes reflected the dim light, making them appear as if they were shining.

The stress from the last day wrapped itself around him. With each step he took toward the fake woman, his anxiety grew to the point where he saw black lines floating across his field of vision.

After removing the velvet rope, he glanced at the table with a worn leather bag in the center. When he grabbed the strap, he thought someone whispered, "Leave it."

Anxiety rippled across his skin, going from boiling hot to freezing cold. Shivering, his head snapped up, and the mannequin's smiling face appeared to twitch.

"Get it together. Vivian needs this." The words echoed as he stared at the plastic woman's red lips, hoping they wouldn't move.

After a few seconds, he unzipped the bag and began rifling through it. The entire time, his back tensed, expecting someone to come from behind and pull him into darkness.

There were assorted jars and tubes with handwritten labels: dog, reptile, youth, and doll.

Notes from the magician were on a scroll of paper. The sketches beneath the scribbled words made bile rise in his throat. Each drawing was of limbs or parts of the anatomy, making it seem like a medical journal. Looking away into the corner, he saw a tiny man propped on a stool. The ventriloquist's dummy appeared to stare through Mike.

His heart was pounding as he pushed the papers aside. A cheap wand was at the bottom of the bag, and next to it was a jar labeled "transformation powder."

The lid was tight. It felt as if it were glued on. After struggling, he finally got it open. Inside was what looked like caked powder that smelled of incense, reminding Mike of church candles.

Mike slipped the small jar into his pocket. Looking around the enclosed area, the mannequin seemed to be moving closer. Her high-heeled feet were only inches away from him now. His thoughts were moving so fast that it hurt to think. He slowly stepped back and tumbled over a chair, landing next to a wooden box shaped like a coffin.

With its arms and fingers reaching out in an awkward gesture, the mannequin rocked back and forth. He saw life in the now-blinking eyes as the female form stumbled, falling toward him. Rolling into the aisle, he got to his feet. He was no longer thinking. It was as if fear was controlling him now.

Watching the mannequin's arms slowly stretch out, he sprinted away, trying to shake the sense that someone was grabbing at the back of his jacket. Reaching the stairs, he bounded down as fast as he could, too terrified to look back. Finally making it to the rear exit, he ran down the alley.

Back at the station, the psychiatrist told him they had made no progress. Mike pleaded with Bradley. It took some coaxing, but she finally agreed to at least attempt to bribe the man with the powder. Mike was sitting on the same bench as before, staring in agony at the door. At first, he heard the clown's shrill laughter. Then, over the last few minutes, there were only muffled voices and a shuffling of chairs.

After fifteen minutes, Bradley came out, with all the color missing from her face. Like a zombie in a cheaply made film, she held up a single finger to Mike and got on her phone as she walked toward him. Barking orders to send an ambulance somewhere on Kedzie, she made eye contact with Mike.

He stood. "Did you find her? Is she okay?"

Putting the phone back in her pocket, she said, "We'll know in a few minutes. I'm sending a squad to the location right now."

"That son of a bitch. What'd he do to her?" Mike stepped past her, heading to the interrogation room, intent on beating him to get the clown to speak. She reached out with her arm and spun him around. He had nearly eighty pounds on her, yet she controlled him as if he were a small child.

"You can't go in there."

Her look froze him. "Why?"

"It's a crime scene now."

"Did you..." He wiggled free from her grip. "Wait! You killed him to get him to talk? He's the only one who knows where my daughter is!"

"No, Mike, it was suicide." She shook her head, her disheveled hair covering part of her face. "I gave him the jar. He laughed that shrill laugh and then gave me the address. Then... he ..." Her hand clasped her mouth, taking a gasping breath. "Mike, the clown put the powder on his face... and then turned skeletal."

"What?"

"I know, it's insane, but believe me, it happened. We have it on camera." She stepped to the side, nodding. "Don't enter, but look for yourself."

Tingling all over, Mike took a hesitant step forward. Inside the small room, bones poked out of the lunatic's clothes. "Holy shi—"

Bradley's phone rang before he could ask any more questions.

"Yes." She nodded as her forehead became a web of lines. "You're sure?" Her eyes grew wide. "Don't touch it. Understand. Nobody touches it until I get there. Lock down the scene. No one enters."

Seeing someone in authority rattled, Mike nearly shouted, "What is it? Is Viv okay?" Her eyes darted from left to right. Taking a deep breath, she said, "I think she can be."

"What does that *mean?*"

She placed her hand on his shoulder. "Mike, this is going to be tough to hear." Thinking of Vivian, he spat, "Tell me!"

"I know this is crazy, but that man told me he changed her into a doll so he could leave her alone without her escaping." She closed her eyes before continuing. "Until I just saw him turn into a skeleton, I thought he was insane..."

"What? Are you saying he turned my girl into a doll?"

The mannequin's smiling face flashed through his thoughts. He was missing something. This couldn't be, even though both his gut and his mind told him he knew the truth. The rumors might not be false. Balzar could perform magic. If this were true, life would never be the same again, regardless of hope or desire.

"I don't really know. The thing is, the officers on the scene say the only thing in the room is a doll wearing the clothes Vivian was abducted in. The doll matches her description, Mike." She pulled out the jar from her back pocket. "He said this could save her. We need to try it. I don't know what else to do."

Mike stood frozen. All he could think of was the sad look on the mannequin's face in the museum and the article. Then, he knew what he'd read had to be real—he could actually perform magic.

Frantically massaging the backs of his hands, he desperately wanted to run away from reality, trying to hide from the fear that was devouring him. When Bradley tugged his arm, he slowly followed her as he wept, hoping Balzar's final magic trick could make his daughter whole again.

HOW LOVELY ARE THY BRANCHES

Whoever is reading this, please heed my warning! I'm writing this locked in the shed, surrounded by something I can't understand. I hope what I'm experiencing is a reaction to whatever I inhaled because if not, whoever enters this forest will be in danger from the monster stalking me.

Darci sat in the window seat of the cabin her father had rented over the Christmas holiday. Flipping through a faded snowmobile manual she'd found in the storage shed, with handwritten notes in every blank space, she assumed what she was reading was a joke.

Tilting her head to the side, she examined the scribbling. With a chuckle that died in the silence surrounding her, she went through the pages. About halfway through, she read, *From the pile of snot, I saw what looked like a tiny man emerge.*

Cringing, she tried to come up with a reason why anyone would write something so odd.

The vibration of her phone made her flinch and then jump enough that she banged her knee against the window.

"Ughhhh." She rubbed her hand across her jeans, feeling like they were dirty after touching the pamphlet, and grabbed her phone.

> *how r things off in the gr8 outdoors*

Seeing Jess's message lightened the mood, which was growing darker by the minute.

Quickly, she typed:

> *bored!*

As she waited for the response from her closest friend, she peered out into the vast darkness. Watching new snow add layers over the already-heavy covering brought an overwhelming sense of isolation. Each new flake erased any remaining color from the dense forest surrounding the old cabin in an arctic cocoon.

> *well, what did u think was going 2 happen*

> *don't know*

> *i just felt bad for my dad*

She started to type *he doesn't have much going for him*. Quickly, she deleted the words. Darci told Jess everything, but since the divorce, a false sense of pride had taken over, making her want to build him up every chance she could, whether it was warranted or not. It oddly alleviated the guilt she felt for choosing to live with her mom, although Darci knew he needed her more.

> *again it's not ur fault ur parents got divorced*

> *i know*

hows the cabin

hmmmmm rustic! i mean, there's indoor plumbing. not much else. i'm surprised I'm still getting a signal

what r you doing tonight

well every year since I was little we'd make popcorn and trim the tree with it so we r supposed 2 do that

supposed 2

my dad's kinda passed out

srsly!! drinking

yeah but it's not like that, really he went out and tried to cut down a tree I think it did something 2 his asthma since he came back, hes been heaving and his face was all blotchy he drank some whisky and said 2 wake him up in an hour

and

He looks so content I figured I would let him sleep some more.

Pulling the dense drape that ran the length of the window seat to the side, Darci looked into the great room toward her father's erratic snoring. It was getting louder, echoing against the wood paneling, reminding her of having to coax him off the couch most nights when he still lived with them. He worked twelve-hour days to make ends meet, but no matter how tired he was, he always insisted on spending his evenings with her, watching whatever silly movies she wanted. He never lasted more than a few minutes before dozing off, but his being that close always made her feel fortunate to have him as a father.

These memories floating through her mind on a night that was meant to be spent surrounded by loved ones increased the sense of homesickness that had been growing since he had picked her up that morning. She was doing her best not to think about it, but she missed her mom. More than that, she missed feeling like a child, being at home playing make-believe, and seeing her parents together; nights like tonight were special. Feelings of loss of something valuable and the sense that everything was slipping away had been haunting her over the last few months.

Darci settled into the window nook nestled between a thick drape and a large window, and curiosity mixed with the right amount of boredom drew her back to the journal. Pulling her knees nearly to her chest, she could smell sap from the tree that her father had tried to cut down, which now seemed permanently stuck to her hands. She grabbed the pamphlet, and a hint of cool air came in as the wind bounced off the thin pane. Wondering if anyone else felt this alone on Christmas, she read on, squinting at the poor penmanship.

When I got back from a walk in the forest, a four-foot tree had somehow sprouted in the middle of the main path to the cabin. I know how improbable that sounds, but I guarantee it wasn't there two hours ago. It looked like a Christmas tree, but the branches were a golden color with a silky texture.

The more I stared at it, the more I realized I had to be mistaken, as there was no way anything could grow that large in such a short time. The tree was obscuring the view from the back window of the cabin, adding to my confusion, as I surely would have noticed it earlier. Perplexed, I was still intent on removing it, so I went to the shed, found garden shears, and came back to the tree. I furiously squeezed and tugged to no avail. The sharp edges didn't even dent the branches. Either this sapling of a tree was petrified, or the shears didn't work. To test the theory, I walked a few steps toward the woods and came across a leafless branch. It was a good two inches in diameter, twice the thickness of the tree I was trying to remove. It took some force, but the shears clipped the branch clean.

Perplexed, after a quick trip back to the shed to get an axe, I stood in front of what was beginning to feel like my nemesis. I swung the axe into the stalk, and it bounced off, making my palms ache in a way I didn't think was possible. Angrier than I should have been, I tossed the axe to the side, firmly grabbed the tree with both hands, and pulled with all I had.

The base did not move, but my hands slipped upward and pulled across the branches, shooting seeds in every direction. I slipped, falling on my backside. If that wasn't bad enough, I took in a big breath full of the tiny seeds, inhaling a few of them. As I sat there dry heaving, the stalk waved slowly back and forth like a pendulum, mocking me. Even then, long before I was attacked, a warning bell went off deep inside that I was dealing with something that had agency. Something that was greater than oneself.

The black ink had red splotches obscuring a few of the letters. Adjusting to make the thin cushion in the window alcove more comfortable, Darci looked through the falling snow to the path she believed the person was describing. It was littered with her and her father's footsteps from finding a suitable tree. The prints were the only blemish in the sea of white. With a huge gust, the wind picked up, howling through the trees and shaking the snow free. She knew she should stop reading. Her nerves were stretched enough that she felt a fluttering in her stomach, yet she read on.

Determined, I finally decided to take a chainsaw to the tree. Just before I was about to get the stalk that plagued me, I lifted the devastating-looking tool, and oil dripped out. The ground was sloped, and the spill slowly made its way toward the tree. When it got close, it seemed to lean away from the petroleum stream like a monster from a torch.

It was the second craziest thing I had seen in the last twenty-four hours. Using a fallen branch, I soaked the edge and used it as a spear, poking firmly at the point where the axe had struck. The tree dodged the spear, and with each jab, it bent away from the oil. Honestly, it looked like it was dancing as it bent and weaved. Amazed, I pulled the cord and took the chainsaw to the trunk. The second the chain made contact, I believe the tree screamed.

Whoever finds this, I know how that sounds, but I swear the tree screamed like a wounded animal. Confused, I kept going, ignoring what had to be a phantom noise. The chain continued to bounce off the skinny stalk, barely making a dent.

As I worked furiously, trying to make progress, an unseen force was obstructing my airway. It was like something had crawled down my throat, and the tail of some small creature was tickling the back of my tongue. Panicked, I tried to cough or scream, quickly realizing I couldn't do either. I clutched at my throat, thinking I could coax the obstruction out. With great force, I finally took a gasping breath. The relief was quickly followed by a violent sneeze that shot out the phlegm that was choking me. The snot pile was almost the same shape as the seeds I had torn off the tree earlier. As I stood, still gasping for air, I saw the unbelievable.

> Mom's drunk already

The text startled Darci so much that she clutched her chest, digging her nails into her hand.

> It's cute and gross at the same time

> She always flirts with my uncle

> I swear she would have been happier with him

Darci felt nearly drunk herself—lightheaded but without any pleasure. Although she was cold, sweat was beading on her forehead. She contemplated texting her friend about what she was reading but simply responded:

> thats really weird

> yeah, it is! u wake up ur old man yet

> no going to soon

> do it already!

> KK

> got to get back to the fun

Despite the building dread, she went back to the story, her heart hammering, hoping to find an admission that this was all a joke or the fiction of a very bored person who had previously stayed there.

From the pile of snot, I saw a very small man emerge. He was covered in the gooey mess. Stretching as if he had just woken from a long nap, he stood and shook like a dog, shooting the snot in every direction. He couldn't be more than two inches tall and was completely nude. His midsection was pudgy, and he had a beard the same silver color as the thin hair atop his round head. After cleaning himself, he ran and leaped over a fallen tree, disappearing into the forest. In a daze, I dusted myself off and went inside, assuming I was suffering from heat exhaustion, a contact high from something in the seeds, or a mixture of both.

After some whiskey, it was becoming easier to ignore the thought of the little man. At that point, I had convinced myself that I most definitely had let my imagination get the better of me, the alcohol making it easier with every sip. Well into the bottle, I guess I passed out because I woke up in the pitch-black front room. Sore from the yard work, I made my way to the kitchen to hunt down some aspirin, with my head pounding enough that thoughts of the little man were the furthest thing from my mind. That is, until I got there.

The kitchen floor, which was less than eight feet from the couch I had been sleeping on, was covered in mud and oil droplets. Fighting panic, I ran through the room, searching for every light switch. I grabbed the largest butcher knife I could find and contemplated calling the sheriff. I was scared, but not quite scared enough to face the embarrassment of calling in hysterically just to find out a raccoon, or some other woodland creature, had made its way in.

Following the path, it led to the front door. Carefully, I moved along the hardwood floor to the window beside the front door. My car had been vandalized. All four tires were flat, and the hood was raised, exposing hanging wires. It was then I noticed what I first thought was a tree next to the front door that hadn't been there before. Leaning further to my right, I saw the third weirdest thing in the last twenty-four hours.

Across the room, Darci heard her father coughing loudly. "Dad?"

She listened, only hearing the wind attacking the window she was leaning against. She squinted, looking toward the couch her father was on. It was hard to make out anything in the room, as there was only a single-bulb lamp in the entire space. Apparently, out in the middle of nowhere, the residents went to sleep when the sun went down.

Fear was willing her to get up and leave—to simply shake her father awake and convince him to get out of this place. She took a deep breath, trying to quiet her thoughts. Needing an anchor to another person, she texted:

hey how's the party?

She stared desperately at the screen, willing a reply. Seconds felt like minutes. Her father's deep snore resumed. Her fingers tapped the face of the phone. Adjusting the turtleneck under her sweater, she picked up the instruction book. It reeked of oil. Knowing she had to find out what was going on, she resumed.

The tree that I had attempted to cut had formed into the shape of a man. Someone had twisted the branches, making them appear like a thick cord, into arms, legs, and torso without a head. The tree man stood nearly five feet tall, and at its waist, it held an axe. It was the axe I had tried to use to chop it down. As if this wasn't enough to terrify me, without any kind of warning, I felt a sharp pain in my big toe.

Pulling my attention from the deadly display, I looked down to see the mucus man holding my Swiss Army knife. It was taller than him, but his ridiculously muscled body handled it very well. He had taken the smallest blade and pierced the middle of my big toe hard enough to go clean through, giving it the appearance of a split tongue. Screaming in pain, fear, or both, I kicked with my intact foot at the booger man and immediately fell forward, the slickness of the oil making me move at twice the speed that I would have thought possible.

Trying to brace myself, I put both hands forward and nearly crushed the tiny bastard. At the last minute, he nimbly dodged me, giving me an unwanted view of his bare behind. I struck the hardwood with a thud.

During his daring escape, the little snot dropped his knife. He now stood stark naked about a foot from my face. I reached my hand up to smash him, and just as I did, he called out in a shrill, unintelligible language. Whatever he screamed, the tree axe murderer certainly understood it, because it instantly burst through the door, wielding the dull axe. Each step looked as if it would be the tree thing's last, yet it kept coming at me.

I no longer had any doubts about hallucinating or had any reasonable explanation. I knew one thing for sure: if I didn't get moving, that axe-wielding maniac was going to split me in half the same way

I had attempted to do to him. I rolled away, somersaulting into a full sprint, heading toward the back door. I had neither a weapon, a phone, nor transportation. Amazingly, in all of this, I still had some logic. I guess it is the fate of an engineer always to be reasonable, even if one of your boogers is trying to kill you by orchestrating a tree killer! I finally made it out the back door, heading to the shed.

It might have been the right choice if there was more oil in here, as that was the only thing that it showed any fear toward. Now, all I have is this can of spray lubricant to protect myself. Every few minutes, the treelike hand snakes through the bottom of the door. I spray it every time, and it recedes. I haven't seen the snot man, but I hear him crying out, hidden within the darkness. I guess he is the brains to the tree's brawn, and he is telling it how to finish me off. I know how ridiculous this sounds, but I've got a theory that the seeds mixed inside me, and it formed the little man. I guess I'll find out either way, because that last spray was more air than oil. Whoever finds this note, if you come across Christmas trees the color of

The writing trailed off into dried red blotches, obscuring the remaining words. Darci googled the cabin's address. Scrolling through advertising for rental information, she saw a news article. There was a picture of a middle-aged man, and the title read, "Engineer Reported Missing." Scanning the article, she read that the man had stayed in the cabin eight months before. The police investigated, finding his car vandalized, and there had been drops of blood and oil on the ground. Mr. Raybury, for now, was presumed missing, and the investigation, although producing evidence suggesting foul play, did not have a suspect. Raybury was divorced and had no children.

Staring at the photo of the very average-looking man, Darci heard her father begin coughing violently, followed by his gasping. The strange noises in the unfamiliar space made her shake. Dropping the pamphlet, she quickly stood to go to him, using her phone light to cut through the darkness. As the beam arched across the small space, she saw that the floorboards had been darkly stained with reflective fluid.

Her heart quickly sped up.

A loud, rustling noise made her point the light in the corner. A jagged shadow of a remarkably thin headless man shuffling near her appeared on the wall.

From behind, there was a shrill cry. Before she could scream, the shadow came forward, revealing a glistening axe.

A CHOICE IN THE MATTER

Anne stared angrily at the man behind the plexiglass, wishing she was somewhere else. It was Thanksgiving, and her notoriously poor planning had her in a bus terminal, waiting for a bus that she suspected would never show.

The fragile man jammed behind the dirty partition, reading the novel *Something Wicked This Way Comes*, had given up placating her. He wouldn't even pretend to radio the driver on their status anymore. Sitting next to her was her four-year-old daughter, who persistently stared at her through thick glasses. Anne almost wished Tina would cry or whine. It would be better than looking at those sad eyes, disappointed at being forced to visit grandparents she barely knew.

Anne knew she should feel blessed to have a well-behaved child, but at this moment, she would give a month's rent to stop being stared at. It was her own fault. She had left Tina's backpack full of books and toys at the apartment in her rush to get there.

"Honey, do you want to play on my phone?"

"Mom, remember, your battery is at ten percent. Since you forgot the charger, don't you think we should save it?"

Anne smiled, wondering how she had managed to keep up with the most responsible kindergartener ever, considering she was barely keeping her own life together. She moved Tina's bangs to the side, thinking how much her daughter was like her late husband. "How about one of these?" She gestured to the small table with magazines littering it. One had a cover with a pop star showing more cleavage than should be allowed. Anne flipped it over. Underneath was a black-and-white magazine about half the size of a comic book. Handwritten across the top was *Amazing Mazes*. Beneath the title was a collection of crooked lines making a maze. At the top right was an arrow saying "Start," and in the center was a heart that said "Finish." Hopeful, she lifted it off the table, which looked as if it had never been cleaned.

Thumbing through the tattered magazine, she saw that none of the mazes had been completed. "Here, honey! You love these things."

Tina, using her index finger, pushed her glasses firmly to her face, making her eyes look even wider. As she looked inside, she had a small, crooked smile. "Pen?"

Anne pulled a stubby pencil from behind her ear. Triumphant, she handed it to her daughter.

Tina quickly began tracing the lines, with her face inches from the paper. Anne's phone vibrated, startling her. Sighing, she answered, "Yes, Mom."

"Are you on your way yet?"

"No." There was a disapproving grunt. Anne pulled her hair into her mouth and nibbled. "Well, I can't hold dinner forever!"

"As I texted you, eat already. We're no strangers to leftovers." She heard her mom mumble under her breath, "I bet."

"When do you think you'll get here?"

"I really couldn't say." Glancing down at the maze book, her heart fluttered long enough that she clutched her chest. The lines Tina had navigated seemed to spell out *Grandma's calling*. Anne knew it was an odd coincidence, but her nervous system would not cooperate with her brain. She turned her head sideways to see how the continuous line could spell out something so strangely specific.

"Anne?"

Her mother's voice pulled her from darker thoughts. It felt as if someone had ratcheted up the heat. Sweat beaded under her hair at the base of her neck. "I ... The ride's three hours, so it depends on when the driver gets here." She watched as Tina moved on to another maze.

Mimicking Anne, she was chewing on her hair as she concentrated on the path. "You should've come this morning."

"I told you I had to work."

"The diner could get by one day with one less waitress."

There was venom in her words that nobody except her daughter would ever detect.

Refusing to be led down that path, she said, "I've got to go. I'll text you when we get moving." Tina was finishing the maze. The continuous line now spelled out *Go to the restroom.*

Anne glanced around the lobby. It was still just them and the station attendant. Instinct compelled her to pull the magazine away from Tina.

"Mom!"

Ignoring her, Anne looked at the back cover. There was no publisher, address, or website, only wording spelling out *Hope you play again soon.* Her fingertips trembled as she realized this was not a mass-produced book, but most likely put together by an amateur. Thinking of the strange mind that would take the time to create it, she flipped through, looking for some clue as to how it got there.

"Mom, no fair." Tina leaned across her lap, trying to grab back the book.

Pulling it further from her grasp, she said, "Tina Beans, let's find something else for you, huh?"

"I like the mazes, Mom."

"Well, let's see if there's something better."

"Why can't I use *that* book?"

Ignoring her, Anne went through the scant magazine pile, finding nothing suitable. An overwhelming urge to get out of the room tickled her nerve endings. Tapping on the linoleum floor with her heels, she stared out at the flurries that were rapidly turning into large flakes. Sweat was dripping down the back of her dress.

Looking up at the man behind the desk, no longer caring whether she aggravated him, she got up. When she cleared her throat, he looked up over the cover of the paperback. His eyes were deep-set and dark, making him look ill.

"When will the bus to Chicago arrive?"

"Like I told you last time. The driver ain't answering."

She raised the maze book. "Is this yours?"

"No." With a self-satisfied grunt, he raised his own book.

"Sir. Please, have you ever seen it before?"

Without lowering the paperback, he responded, "No."

"You know, pal... " She bit her lower lip, knowing whatever she was about to do would not improve anything. Going back to the bench in the corner, Anne saw Tina frantically digging through Anne's purse.

"I'm thirsty."

Tina had spilled half the contents of Anne's overflowing purse onto the bench. "Uuuuugh, Beans!"

Anne watched as Tina walked the few steps past the washroom to the vending machine. Standing on tiptoes, she carefully inserted the change.

Anne glanced at her buzzing phone. The message was from her mother, saying *sorry*. Rolling her eyes, she looked back up. Tina was gone.

Anne's eyes darted around the room. Her heart was thumping, making it hard to realize that the only place she could have gone was into the bathroom. Looking down, she saw the maze spelled out *Get a drink Tina.* Ignoring the tingling in her fingers, she stood and nearly sprinted to the door.

The dirty room had two stalls, a sink, and a mirror. One stall door was open. The other had large snow boots visible under the metal partition. There was nowhere else for Tina to hide in the tiny space, yet she wasn't there. Anne's heart seemed to rise in her chest, nearing her throat, slowing the air intake enough that tiny black dots floated past her eyes. All her senses came alive. Smelling dirty water and bleach, she stared at the stall door, wanting to kick it open.

Just as she was about to, she realized that in the hour they'd been there, no one else had entered the bus station. Wondering why someone would sit in a bathroom for so long, she squeaked, "Excuse me?"

The boots shifted as the stall door creaked open.

Anne jerked her head back. The woman looked so much like her it was overwhelming.

She wasn't an exact duplicate, but close enough to be her sister. Anne wanted to leave, and adrenaline shot through her, urging her to obey. Fighting to stay calm, she said, "Pardon me." The woman's expression did not change. She looked like a church patron with the hint of a smile and boredom in her eyes.

Anne stepped back, bumping into the sink.

Coming alive, the stranger said, "We don't have much time." The woman took a single step forward, filling the stall's opening.

Every nerve ending was taut, dancing inside. "What?" Anne tilted her head, looking into the small stall. Frantically, she said, "Have you seen a little girl? Please, you must have seen something!"

The woman grabbed the end of her hair and started chewing. "Mom, please listen to me."

"What?" A connection was made deep inside, where reason didn't quite reach emotion.

She saw Tina in the woman's face. Anne stepped slowly toward the door, her temples throbbing in waves. "Who're you?"

Emerging from the shadow, the woman put on thick glasses. With a crooked smile, she said, "It's me, Mom." She raised her head and showed a tiny scar in the shape of a flying bird beneath her jaw.

"Remember when I was a kid... I mean, last year when the swing hit me?"

Anne looked at the scar; her stomach ached as she remembered the day it happened. "We haven't much time. Our paths will only cross like this once. I understand this is difficult. That book I'm playing with will tell us the future. But you must decide if you want to listen to it."

"This's insane." Anne walked to the bathroom door, ripping it open. The lobby was gone. In its place was a maze of tall white walls. "What's happening?" She staggered back, unable to process what she was seeing.

Tina was at her side. "Mom. You are in a time and place that is between both. Whoever created that book opened this world. This brief moment only exists so you can decide what is best for me."

"What's happening, and how do you know this?"

"Because I've lived the life the book has provided me." She stepped closer. "This's my future. I'm alone but safe and just getting by." Her lips worked over the strand of hair. "The messages in the book stopped me from ever taking a risk. It may have improved things, but it also stopped me from being more. I've always followed the writing until now."

Anne took a step forward, touching the maze wall. Like a movie playing in her head, she saw Tina going to the prom. Fear made her legs weak as she stepped back into the bathroom. "What was that?"

"Pieces of my future."

Massaging her hand, Anne said, "Where am I? In this... future?"

A tear ran down Tina's cheek. "I can't answer any questions, as it can alter your decision."

"What decision?"

"If you follow that maze, you can get back to the younger me. When you do, you won't remember any of this. All you will know is what your feelings tell you. You have to decide if I should keep following the messages or live a life that's not predestined."

"This's insane." She reached out and touched Anne's face. Her flesh was as cold as ice.

Recoiling, she said, "Why am I given this choice?"

"If you choose to keep it, the book will answer that question." Closing her eyes, Tina whispered, "You must go now, before it's too late." She pushed Anne toward the maze.

Feeling dizzy, she stepped forward, hearing the door close behind her. When she reached to open it, the door disappeared, becoming part of the maze. Brushing the wall, she saw Tina crying to a man, begging him not to leave her. With her arms pinned to her sides, Anne walked forward, trying to avoid the f uture.

Each step echoed against the walls, mixing with a whisper from the same voice surrounding her.

Mom, where are you? Mom, I got into college!

Anne covered her ears, causing her elbow to brush the immovable wall. There was an image of a coffin. Before she could see who was in it, she pulled back. Clutching her aching chest, she ran up and down the narrow corridor sideways. Coming to multiple dead ends, she frantically retraced her steps. Every time she touched the walls, she saw another moment of Tina's life.

Finally, there was a sliver of light ahead and the shadow of a little girl. Winding around the corner, she saw a narrow opening to the lobby of the bus terminal. As she took the last step, she closed her eyes.

The Tina she knew was leaning over the maze book. With a deep sigh, Anne sat next to her daughter.

Anne, for a moment, couldn't remember where she was. Confused, she felt her own forehead. Feeling a heaviness like she never had in her life, she glanced at the book, reading *Keep me in a safe place Tina.*

The man at the counter called, "Hey, lady, bus's here."

Frightened, Anne grabbed their suitcase. When she touched Tina's hand, she saw an older woman's face on her body. Startled, she jerked away, and Tina instantly looked like herself.

Disoriented, she pulled her daughter toward her, frantically taking the book. "Beans, that's not for you." As they left, Anne tossed the book onto the dirty table, feeling as though she had done this all before.

DUPLICATE

Deep down, Ray knew the odd-looking man he was staring at was an imposter. He'd been ruminating on him since he first saw him at the funeral earlier that day. Ray scooted over on the couch and looked away from the man whom he'd seen at every major family event since he was a young boy. Nudging the elderly woman beside him, he said, "Tell me again, what's the deal with Iblis? Is he a cousin?"

"Which one is he?"

"Over on the wingback chair with the curly wig. When we were young, you made us call him 'cousin.'"

"Oh, yes, yes, I remember him now. No, he isn't your cousin." She stared at Ray for a few seconds as if he were a stranger. Her face went slack. "When we all came here from Yugoslavia, his father let us stay rent-free in his apartment building until we could find jobs. So, in a way, he is more than family. It forged the relationship between all of us in caring, not just blood."

"Granny, that's a funny way to put it." Ray smiled and patted her leg. She pulled away slightly and gave him an awkward look. Ignoring the eccentricity of the woman, who was quickly approaching the centenarian mark, he asked, "What's his deal, though?"

Someone flipped on the radio. The sound made the room quieter, as if the partygoers preferred the quiet, dull opera music over the conversations with family members they rarely saw.

"What do you mean *deal*?"

"Why is he always alone? He never talks to anyone. He just sits in the corner by himself. Kinda odd, considering he's family." He tried to remember a single time the man had contributed to any event in his family's history other than just showing up, coming up with nothing.

"I couldn't say. Have you ever tried asking him?"

"I've never talked to him beyond 'hi' and 'bye' and overhearing some obligatory small talk. Frankly, the guy gives me the creeps."

With a curved arthritic hand, she slapped at him playfully. "Do you have to be so mean?"

"Well, no. But look at him. He wears that weird rug on top of his head, and it looks like he is wearing makeup. It scares me a little being around him, like he'll try to touch me inappropriately or something."

"It's not polite to joke like that." She raised her hand, covering the beginning of a smile. "Okay, but I'm not really joking."

It was as if the odd man had been summoned from across the room. He scanned the crowd and made eye contact with Ray. Slowly, the man put his hand to his nose and appeared to move it half an inch to the right as if he were a clay figurine. The entire time, his expression never changed.

"Seriously, was he in an accident or something?" Ray cringed as he watched the man apparently reposition his flesh.

"Not that I'm aware of."

"How old is he?"

"Well." She twisted her lips, adding to the web of wrinkles over her face. "That's a good question. Seems like, in all of my memories, he's always been an adult. But that can't be right, can it? Or he'd be much older than me. He certainly doesn't look it."

The man smiled and then turned his head slightly to the right, appearing to be staring at the blank wall, seeing something that apparently only he could recognize.

"Well, you have to remember something more than that. Did he ever give you a gift or invite you over?"

"I'm very tired. I don't usually stay up this late, and all that food!" She rubbed her belly, smiling. "I don't eat like that very often anymore."

Ray grinned despite the frustration of not getting answers. He couldn't help himself.

Whenever he saw her smile, it brought back so many memories of his childhood and of her many acts of kindness. There was no stopping it. "You want some cake?"

"No, no way. Got an appointment with my doctor in the morning. Don't want to have to explain my blood sugar. He's a tyrant!"

"Well, I want some, so if you'll excuse me, I'll catch up with you later."

"Come see me before you go, Liebchen."

"Okay." Ray got off the couch, which was so worn and low to the floor that he struggled to stand. He walked across the room, smiling at mourners he barely recognized, and hoped they wouldn't try to pull him into an awkward conversation. Why was the morbid custom of gathering and eating after a burial so widely adopted? He wished these gatherings were at night, and everyone would immediately part in solitude after. It seemed a more fitting tribute. Trying to sugarcoat death with polite conversation seemed to diminish the significance of what was happening.

Approaching the food table, he saw in the corner of his eye the cousin mouthing words to no one. Ray fought the impulse to confront the man, but his last conversation with this grandmother had been so awkward that he wasn't up for another.

Grabbing a paper plate with a slice of cake on it, he walked up to his younger sister. "You want to do something peculiar after we leave here?" Biting into the frosting that tasted like cardboard, he winced, wondering who would make such an obnoxious dessert. He tossed the plate into the overflowing trash.

"Ummm, always."

"Good."

"Well. What is it?"

"We're going to follow Cousin Iblis home."

His sister laughed deeply, exposing the stud in her tongue, which she usually concealed from the family. Quickly, she covered her mouth with her hand, her black nail polish glistening. "Why?"

"Because I need to know more about him."

Her right eyebrow raised as she asked, "Dude, what's up with you?"

"We see that man at weddings, funerals, and other major family events. I'm not even sure he's even a relation, and whenever he shows up, I ask around, and nobody ever remembers inviting him. Every family member has a different story of how he's related. How can that be?"

"You're acting weird, Bro." She twirled her finger in circles at her temple and opened her eyes very wide.

"Maybe."

She chuckled. "Well, instead of playing Sherlock, why don't you just ask him where he lives?"

"Mom did once in her usual hospitable way. I think she told him it was for a Christmas card or some shit."

"And?" She drew the word out, raising her eyebrows. "He gave her the address of a subway terminal."

"Admittedly odd, but really, who cares?"

"It's not easy to explain, but I need to know."

"Did he touch you funny when you were younger? Do you need me to bring you a doll to show where?" She patted him on the shoulder, faking a look of concern.

"That's not funny. Not at all." Even though he'd made a similar joke, the thought brought a tingle down his back. Every time he was near the man, he sensed something less than wholesome was driving him.

"Oh, lighten up."

"Hey, I'm perfectly light." Ray shook his head quickly. "Well, you know what I mean. Look, I won't follow him out to the boonies or anything. I figured he'd either take a cab or an EL train. Whole thing can't take more than half an hour or so. If I can get an address, I might figure out who he really is. For all we know, he might be some kind of psycho party crasher."

"That's an overly dramatic statement, Raymond." After a loud sigh, she added, "I'll go, but I still think you're obsessing way too much over nothing. Ever since you turned twenty-four, you've been getting weirder and weirder."

"I've been asking questions about this guy for well over two years now. Nobody knows where he lives, how old he is, or if he has any other family besides ours. He always looks the same age in any pictures I've dug up of him."

"It's that bad toupee. Put that on, and you wouldn't look like you ever changed either. The eyes are instantly drawn to it, making it hard to focus on anything else." She tilted her head and stood on her tiptoes, glaring at the man. "You know, speaking of eyes, his kinda looks like yours. Cloudy and bright at the same time."

"Whatever. Just pay attention. When he leaves, we leave, okay?"

"Sure thing."

The sense that something was very off was growing oppressive as Ray made his way to the liquor table.

An hour later, Emma was nowhere to be found, and Ray was slowly walking down the stairs of the brownstone, trying not to be spotted by the old man. The man's step had an odd hitch that looked as if his right side were heavier than his left. Watching him fight the stairs, Ray wondered what caused it.

The night air was cold enough to make Ray wish he'd worn long underwear. His dress pants did little to keep off the biting wind. With every step, he hoped Iblis would grab a cab. Then, at least, he could tail him with a heater nearby.

As they made their way down State Street, Ray was stunned that the man could handle the weather. He was only wearing a wrinkled dress shirt and slacks. Staring at the clothing made Ray shiver. Keeping enough distance to not be obvious, he watched as the man turned the corner on Heron, heading east.

Before long, the streets were alive with late-night bar hoppers. They were ducking in and out of cabs, huddling in dark club entrances as they were just beginning their night.

The man slowed and looked up at a tall building that had a Starbucks and a deli at the ground level. Watching him, Ray walked to the sewer grate and stood over it, feeling the heat.

After a few seconds, the man began moving again. One step, hitch, and then another step. Ray reluctantly moved from the steam, following, when something clutched at both his sides.

He spun, imagining it was the old man. Instead, his sister stood laughing hysterically. "Oh, you should see your face right now." She tented her fingers, bringing them to her smiling mouth. "Oh, soooo good."

"Not funny!" Ray put his hand on his chest, feeling the throbbing against it.

"Don't be a baby. It was funny."

Taking a sharp breath in, he asked, "Where were you?"

"When I saw your man of mystery leaving, I scooted out to get ahead of you." Raising his eyebrows, he nearly yelled, "Just to scare me?"

"Pretty much." She smiled. Nodding her head down the street, she said, "Hey, we better keep up before AARP over there gets away from us."

Ray turned, his eyes following the man sauntering away with his same repetitive cadence.

Slowly, they followed as the wind whipped past them, pushing trash along the gutters.

In her low heels, Emma fought to keep up with her brother. Loudly, she blurted out, "This time of year sucks."

"Yeah."

"Too cold, and no real events to look forward to."

"Valentine's Day is an event."

"Yeah, if you are a twit."

He chuckled. "Thanks for coming. I appreciate it, even if you nearly gave me a grabber."

"Told you I would go."

"Yeah. Then disappeared. Nothing unusual there."

"Don't start."

Ray let the conversation drop, as he was not in the mood for a fight. They walked along, struggling against the wind as it picked up the closer they got to the lake. The old man trudged along, seemingly oblivious to everything around him. The evening was growing darker the farther they got away from the Loop and the lights of the stores.

Everywhere Ray looked, shadows seemed to play tricks with his mind. Each perceived threat tensed his nerves.

Focusing on watching the man walk in his strange way was hypnotic. He was like a robot, programmed to never vary from the rhythmic movement. After what seemed like an hour, the man came to a dilapidated building. The two-story structure was dwarfed by the enormous buildings flanking it. Ray thought he could read *Visiting Star Theater* as a dusty impression from a sign removed in the aging brick above the entrance.

His maybe-cousin pulled at a glass door that had been waxed over in soapy swirls. They opened easily without a key.

Ray turned to his sister. "Could there be apartments in there?" He squinted, trying to look through the doors. "It looks like it should be condemned."

She lifted her chin from her scarf. "Doubt it. Maybe he owns the building and is just checking in on it."

"Well, if that's the case, maybe we're due an inheritance when he croaks. A place that big has got to be worth something." He tried to smile, but his lips didn't want to cooperate. Trying to see what was happening inside, he said, "Sit tight at the bus stop. I'm going inside."

"You nuts? If it's an open warehouse, he'll see you the second you walk in."

"I'll be quiet."

"You have an address. That's what you came here for. Let's get a cab and get out of here."

She tugged at his sleeve, her eyes pleading enough to give him a wave of guilt as he saw the redness in her cheeks, but he fought the feeling. "It will only take a minute. Promise."

She gripped his arm. "Dude, you're acting crazy. You're not leaving me out here alone, and I'm sure as heck not going into that creepy-ass building to follow a guy who looks like death."

His heart skipped a beat, hearing exactly what he'd been thinking. Ray looked into his sister's eyes and then back at the building. With a deep sigh, he pushed away the obsessive thoughts spinning inside his head and pulled out his phone. The ride app showed that a car would be there in less than five minutes.

"Might as well not freeze while we wait." He walked to the covered bus stop. One wall had scratched plexiglass. Sitting on the bench, he couldn't shake the feeling that someone was staring at them. They sat close together, huddling for warmth.

Adjusting her hat, she said, "I'm not paying for the ride. Following him was your idea."

"I got it."

"How do you keep going without a real job?"

Her ability to ask anything, regardless of how rude, was a constant annoyance. "I'm doing fine."

"For how long, though?"

"Look. I'm not going to get into this." As their car approached, he felt a sense of relief that he didn't have to explain his lifestyle again. When headlights flashed across the face of the abandoned building, the relief quickly vanished. Through the shadows beyond the frosted windows, Ray thought he saw the man floating inside the vacant building, staring at them. He knew it was either his imagination or a trick of the light. As the car completed the turn, the building went back to darkness, and the dancing shadows disappeared.

The car came to a stop in front of them. Eager to get as far away from the building and its inhabitants as possible, he gripped his sister's arm, pulling her to the car. When they got in, it smelled overwhelmingly of cologne and incense, but it was at least warm. As they cruised along for the first time since he'd left the party, Ray's toes were no longer numb. Wiggling his feet as the blood flowed, he found it wasn't a completely unpleasant stinging.

When his hands warmed, Ray pulled up public records. The page loaded painfully slowly.

After patiently retyping the information, he found that the theater building was owned by Raymond Goodwin. Seeing his own name coursed adrenaline throughout him.

Tingling, he looked at his sister. She was sitting with her eyes closed and her head against a filthy window. He nudged her with his elbow, needing someone to reassure him that the owner having the exact same name could have a logical reason. She swatted him away like a mosquito. As his mind raced, he googled the name of the theater.

The first website was cheap-looking and detailed the forgotten buildings of Chicago. The Visiting Star Theater opened in the early 1900s, and there was a long list of performances that had been put on at the venue.

Ray scrolled to the section on the owner. His name was Raymond Goodwin. He was neither an actor nor a playwright, but had kept the theater going for nearly half a century before it closed. There was a quote from a theater critic who said he'd known Mr. Goodwin for several years and had tried to persuade him to keep the popular cultural hub open. However, for an unknown reason, the owner had refused and was never heard from again.

Scrolling further, he found the owner's picture. Staring into his mirror image, Ray quickly closed his phone.

In a trance, he watched the lights of the city dance off the windows of the cab as sweat coated his upper body. Needing a distraction, he looked upward to hundreds of lit-up windows. He thought of the many inhabitants, wishing he could switch places with them. The thought of warmth and familiarity added to the growing sense of dread that had enveloped him since he'd begun his investigation.

Taking a deep breath, he clicked his phone on and enlarged the picture that had shaken him. It was black and white and heavily pixelated, displaying a group of men and women in ostentatious costumes surrounding a man wearing a bowler hat. Ray knew the picture could have easily been mistaken for him. Even with the poor condition of the picture, every curve of Ray's face was there, including the tiny scar above his right eyebrow from a childhood diving mishap. Frantic, his mind ran through the conversations he'd had with his family regarding Cousin Iblis, wondering what the relation truly was.

He nudged his sister again, this time more forcefully.

In a sharp tone, she squeaked out, "What?" She never opened her eyes.

Feeling squeamish, Ray glanced at the back of the driver's head. More concerned about the rising anxiety than a stranger thinking him insane, he said, "Look at this picture."

"Ughhh." She put both hands on the seat and straightened herself. Blinking several times, she grunted. "Dude looks exactly like you."

"Yeah." He wanted to say more, but couldn't. It was as if his brain was saving all of its energy to combat the rising fear.

"Where's that from, and why does it look all old-timey?"

"It's the owner of the theater we just left."

"Woah." She pulled her head back slowly. "That's freaking spooky."

"I... I think it's Iblis when he was younger."

"Less creepy then. I guess the guy really is related."

"How can he look just like me?"

"Maybe he's your actual dad!" Her eyes were wide, and her mouth hung open, eating up the fun.

Exasperated, he responded loudly, "Seriously, I'm trying to figure this out."

"Bro. I'm serious. Maybe Mom was a slut bag and had an affair with that guy. Could explain a lot."

"Please, this isn't a joke." Maybe if it wasn't an affair, he would be called Ray Goodwin Jr. The thought equally sickened and relieved him, momentarily taking away the thoughts of an unworldly connection.

Emma leaned forward, craning her neck, to look at the street sign. "We're almost to me." She zipped up her jacket. "Don't look so idiotic, Ray. I was just teasing. Maybe you were named after him, and he turned out to be a weirdo, so nobody will tell you that. Beyond that, the guy must be a cousin and just didn't age well. Doesn't mean you'll end up like an uggo wearing a bad rug. Well, with your face, the ugly part could definitely happen, but if you wore a toupee like that, I swear I'd rip it straight off your head and make you eat it."

"Thanks," he sneered. Her attitude was slightly loosening what felt like a band wrapped around his chest. The car jammed to a sudden halt as the driver spun his head around.

"This is you."

"Yeppers." She grabbed her purse, which was the size of a pillbox. "I'll call you in the morning, Raymond."

In a flash, she was out of the cab, letting in a dose of fresh frigid air.

She slammed the door, giving him a stare that told him not to do anything stupid. He fought to grin back as the driver asked in a thick, unrecognizable accent, "Where you heading to?"

Ray stared at the man but didn't see him. He knew this was more than an obsession and doubted whether he'd be able to sleep or concentrate on anything else if he didn't go back. The pull was greater than anything he'd ever experienced. He knew it wasn't right, yet he wanted it anyway.

"Friend, where you headed to?"

"Take me back to the place you just picked us up from."

"Really?"

Ray silently stared at him, ready to snap his head off. The building anxiety needed an anchor. The driver and his stare were the perfect targets.

"All right. It's your dough."

Ray had to know. It felt like every nerve ending in his body was awakening, pointing him in the direction of the theater and the man inside. As the car made a U-turn, Ray thought of all the times he'd seen the man at gatherings and the way he always stared. The pieces were coming into place. It was unlikely, but he considered whether the man could be his father.

Ray had never felt connected to his father, but had always felt a strong kinship toward both his mother and his sister. It didn't come from who they were or how they treated him. It was something much more. When he was with them, it felt right, like they were destined to be together. There was an unexplainable connection that would always be there, regardless of distance or circumstance.

Every time he was around the man that he thought was a distant cousin, he felt something similar. A sense that something larger was drawing him to Iblis. The feeling wasn't as positive as it was with his sister, but the sense of belonging was there, buried among the curiosity and fear.

After a few minutes of tense thought, Ray looked up as the car came to a stop in front of the empty theater. After paying, he jogged across the street, fighting a building wind. The empty streets and surrounding buildings added to the growing desolation that was making it hard to care about anything more than solving the mystery. There wasn't a light in any of the soaped-over windows, making it seem like Ray had wandered into a place where no one belonged. As he sucked in a deep breath between the wind's mighty gusts, the cold rush in his lungs helped take the focus away from the anxiety enough to give him the courage to enter the darkness.

He pushed the door open. Stepping into the blackness, he found it was only slightly warmer inside, with the shield of the aging structure from the wind. The floor was an expanse of unpolished terrazzo littered with old newspapers and other assorted trash. Taking small, tentative steps, Ray walked toward a doorway with a fabric curtain in front of it. There was a small beam of light through the sliver, where the two panels nearly overlapped. Ray thought of turning on the light from his phone but decided not to, worrying it would draw too much attention. Before he entered, he held his breath, waiting to hear something. All that was there was the weather attacking the glass doors. Finding courage, he pulled the thick fabric aside, and dust particles clouded his vision. Covering his mouth with the sleeve of his jacket and squinting, he saw the enormous space that was once a theater but now looked like a graveyard of worn chairs.

A dull, unseen light source made everything in the cavernous room look like a black-and- white movie. Ray stood frozen, carefully studying the space. Everything looked as it had in the pictures, like a time capsule from a time long forgotten. There was ornamental woodwork everywhere he looked. Strewn within the wood were carvings of unrecognizable faces that had to be long gone. The theater had rows and rows of lined fabric seats with carpeted walkways between them.

Ray cupped his hand to his ear, listening for any sign of life. Confident that he was either alone or being watched by someone who didn't want to be discovered, he began walking forward. The floor sloped to an elevated stage. Every footstep echoed in the darkness, the domed ceiling amplifying the creaking of the floorboards. The closer he got to the front, the better he could make out three identical boxes. They looked very old, made of plain wood and large metal hasps.

He looked all around before hopping onto the dusty stage, which caused a thundering sound. Flinching, he looked to the ceiling until the echo died, the whole time expecting Iblis or some creature of the night to come crawling out of the woodwork.

Cautiously moving forward, the farther he got from the lobby, the darker it got, but he knew there was no choice. Figuring whether someone stalking would have come out by now, he pulled out his phone. Using the light, he examined the lettering on the boxes. There were several letters stamped in circles, spelling out words he couldn't read. Stepping back, he realized that they were calligraphy and were in a language foreign to him. Taking a picture, the flash in the dark room made him dizzy enough to wobble.

Shaking the cobwebs out of his head, he jiggled the clasp on the first box. It was shut tight. He shook it up and down, trying to jimmy it open. A metallic clang shot through the theater, reminding him he was on a stage that had been built to project sound in the days before speakers. Flinching again at the sharp echo, there was an overwhelming sense of someone inches behind him.

Giving it one last solid tug, he found the small lock wouldn't budge past the inch the hasp would allow. Moving to the second box, when he touched the lock, it opened in his hand, bringing a feeling of relief and then dread. Pulling the lock free, he put his phone into his pocket to open the lid. The hinge needed oiling. When he peered inside, it was dark enough to give Ray hope that what he saw wasn't actually there.

Inside was his cousin, folded over himself like a rag doll. His appendages were bent in ways that did not seem at all possible, like a discarded marionette. Disoriented, Ray backed away, feeling as if his body were trying to shake free of his skin.

A voice spoke slow and distorted, sounding like an audio recording played at a low speed. "So pleased you finally came, Raymond."

Ray's heel struck a stage light built into the floor. He almost fell backward as he stared at the box. Flailing wildly, he regained his balance and hunched forward. Through the shadows, he saw the man in the box stand like a balloon inflating.

"Oh God." Ray clasped his hand over his mouth, stifling a scream. His fingers reeked of the dust of the theater, making him gag.

"Don't be afraid, Raymond."

Ray's breath felt frozen, leaving him choking on waves of dirty air that stung his lungs.

With a slight wiggle, the man stood fully erect, looking like he had at the funeral. Looking unnatural, but at least now whole, the creature took a step out of the box, hitching and advancing. Once Iblis was free, he straightened the wig on its h ead.

"What are you?" The second the words were out of his mouth, Ray saw the resemblance.

The man without any stage makeup was indeed his mirror image. "I am you."

"But... how?" Ray wanted to close his eyes, but some instinct told him that if he did, the man would leap across the stage and on top of him.

"*Why* would be the more relevant question, Raymond."

"I don't know who put you up to this, but you did your job." Ray forced a laugh. The darkness seemed to steal it from the air. "I'm scared shitless." His bowels whined as if in response.

"I know." The figure extended its arms forward, holding up its palms before continuing in a steady voice. "I am not here to harm you, Raymond."

Every time he heard his name, Ray wanted to scream. The word made his nerve endings taut, and he shivered. Whatever he was staring at shouldn't know anything about Raymond, much less speak his name out loud. Through gritted teeth, he asked, "What do you want from me?"

"For you to do your part."

The man took a small step forward. His frail body was surrounded by dust. The dim light of the room was square on the man's face, making it appear to glow.

"What does that mean?"

"To take my place. Or, should I say, *your* place?"

Raymond's eyes darted to the box and then back to the monster that was slowly advancing. "Never." His response was whispered so quietly that it was as if he didn't want the duplicate to hear and be able to challenge his protest.

"You haven't any choice. Your time is here."

Raymond turned and jumped off the stage. His stride increased with each step he took up the theater's long aisle. There was less light at ground level, making it hard to see more than inches in front of him.

From behind, the voice boomed throughout the room. "If you leave now, you will not make it until morning."

Ray stood still, feeling the adrenaline course through him in waves. He couldn't bring himself to turn and face the man. When he tried, it was as if the signal from his brain was lost somewhere in the panic. He shouted, "What?"

"Your life is no longer yours. Now that you have glimpsed this side, nothing can go back to the way it was."

Ray turned. "What do you want from me?"

"Raymond, your place is here now. It's my time to move on, and for you to take over the space that I once occupied."

Ray brought both hands to the sides of his head, grabbing at his hair, trying desperately to push away the fear that jumbled his thinking. "*What's happening?*" His scream echoed throughout the theater.

"You made a deal some time ago. When your spirit was ready to go, you begged for extra time here in this ..." He stopped and looked down at his body with a disdainful look, laughing at the makeshift costume the spirit had covered itself in. "... flesh. I granted you your request and held off the next world by staying here in this box. Now, it's your turn."

"What are you?"

"I was the ghost who was to guide you to the other side. That is, until we made our deal."

Thinking of how horrible a place the spirit came from had to be to make him want to live a life alone in that box, Ray began to weep.

"We cheated the inevitable, and I've sacrificed so I can once again be among the living.

The only reason no one from the other side has found me is because I have remained half- formed, leaving me as neither a full spirit nor a human. In this state, they can't sense us. This won't last forever, though. Now, you must fulfill your end of the bargain before they catch on."

Ray turned quickly and strode to the lobby. His heart was now moving as fast as his mind. As he made it out of the theater, his steps slowed, and he inched along as he fought flashes of blackness that blurred his vision. The farther he got from the maniac that had come out of the box, the weaker his muscles felt, making it hard to walk. Feeling like he was going to vomit, he wobbled backward, taking a small step toward the theater. Oddly, it slowed down what-

ever mechanism inside him was causing him to feel ill. The nausea pa
ssed.

He took another step toward the theater, and his blurry vision cleared. From inside the vast space, he heard the voice boom, a deep baritone bouncing off the walls, vibrating the room.

"I can't let you leave, Raymond. If you do, I'll have no choice but to go back to my spirit form, and then they will take us both."

Ray struggled to stand still, suddenly tasting copper in his mouth. Fishing his tongue around, he realized he'd bitten his lip hard enough to make it bleed. Concerned he wouldn't stay upright much longer, he grabbed his phone and dialed his sister. After four rings, she answered in a groggy voice.

"Who is this?"

It hurt to speak. The words felt like they were tangible and were scratching the inside of his throat. Almost choking on bile through cascading tears, he said, "It's me, Sis."

"Huh... sorry. I don't recognize your number... or voice. Who?"

"It's Ray, Emma!"

"Buddy, I don't know who you are. Do you have the wrong number?"

"*Wrong number*? Emma, it's your brother." A ring of hope chimed off somewhere deep in his subconscious. She was in on it. This was all a joke.

"Dude, I don't have a brother."

"Emma, it's your older brother, Ray. Please. Please listen."

"You sound like you're in a bad way, and I wish I could help you. I'm nine months pregnant and can hardly get out of bed, pal. Sorry for whatever you're going through. I wish you well. Please don't call me again."

A part of Ray died as the line went silent, and his hope evaporated. Whatever was happening was growing more definite. The suspicion that had been guiding him for the last hour brought a sense of deep sadness. He couldn't understand how, or why, but he knew deep inside himself that there was no going back to his normal life now. He understood this the second he saw the man in that box. The reality of it was dulling the pain, wrapping it in melancholy.

From behind him, the baritone sounded again. "It's your choice, Raymond. If you make it out the door of the theater, you will die a natural death, and I will once again become a spirit and end our shared existence. However, if you come back to me, you will live on."

The reality of the words stung deeply. Ray looked back into the shadow-filled theater, knowing what he would do, even though his body wasn't cooperating. It was like a deep sensor in his brain was trying to protect him.

"Come to me and live on as I have lived. You will at least have a few hours with your family while you wait your turn."

Stepping toward the theater, he screamed, "*Why did you come out at all?*"

"You need to be near your loved ones when they are in a large group to gain energy from them. It's the burden of existing between the two worlds and belonging to neither."

Whimpering, Ray took another step toward the theater. Shuffling along made him feel physically stronger, but also like his heart was torn from his chest. As he got closer, memories of his past life began filling in. He saw a lifetime in seconds, each image replacing his current memories.

Finally, as he remembered his last meeting with the spirit, any sense of humanity was left behind in the lobby, leaving only fear and dread of the inevitable. It seemed to weigh down his steps, yet he kept making the descent to his future life, unwilling to accept the alternative.

A month later, the room was alive with chatter and piano music. Emma was standing in the corner next to her grandmother, holding her newborn.

"Emma, where's the baby's father?"

"Granny, you know you shouldn't ask questions like that." Emma smiled, looking across the room.

Raymond sat in the corner, staring at the child who had taken his place. The anger and longing were there, but they were now a dull throb, like the scar tissue of an old injury. The makeup and wig were in place, making him almost fit in, but he knew the woman whom he'd once called sister was suspiciously eying him. After a few minutes, he'd heard her ask his grandmother who he was. Straining to hear across the room, he leaned forward.

His grandmother, in her slow way of speaking, told a story that she thought he was a distant cousin from the old country. When Emma asked if he was blood-related, he heard Granny respond, "I can't say for sure, but wouldn't you say your son has his eyes?"

Ray desperately wanted to speak. He hadn't yet mastered his new spirit form, so his lips simply wavered as they did in the box when he tried to call out. His life was now relegated to appearing only at sporadic family gatherings, hiding among a group that was too polite to discover what he really was. He wanted to scream and remind his sister of their relationship, but he knew that if he did, it would all be over. Instead, he sat, absorbing these brief moments, knowing that in a few hours, he would be back to the complete darkness of the box.

DARK RIDE

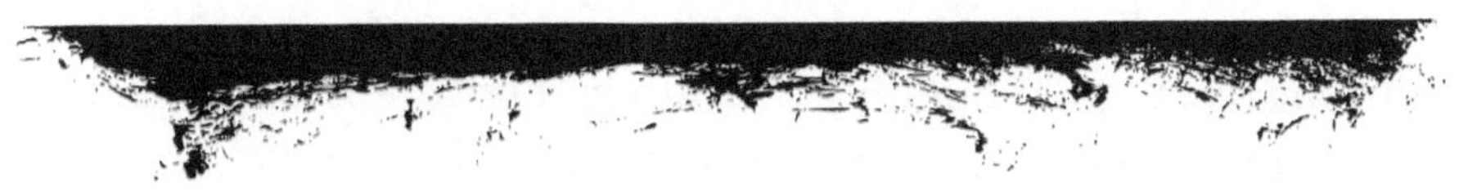

The Demon's dark, glaring eyes, surrounded by flames on the ride's marquee, were now in sight. Navigating his daughter through the crowd, Charlie could see the carnival manager with his bad combover standing on the roller coaster's landing platform. It was difficult to see whether the ride was running or whether the screams were coming from somewhere else in the fairground.

His daughter was tugging so hard at his flannel shirt that Charlie was concerned that the buttons were going to pop loose. Half of her painted-on tiger whiskers were wiped away around her mouth from where she'd been stuffing cotton candy. Shirley, after asking a few dozen times, had made him begrudgingly give in and pay 20 bucks to the carnival rip-off artist, who airbrushed on her favorite animal. The paint was a constant reminder of how little he wanted to be there. Carnivals, to him, were a waste of time and money. The cheap thrill of the rides was hardly worth the wait or expense.

"Daddy! Play that bottle game. I want the big bear." Shirley pointed with sticky fingers to a cheap stuffed bear that was taller than her.

Thinking of her trying to carry it, he smirked. Bending, he adjusted her ponytail, pulling in the strands of hair that were always trying to escape. "Hey, Pumpkin-Butt, maybe later." He had already sunk nearly 40 bucks into similar games with nothing to show for it. Remembering the two unused ride admission tickets they'd left, he asked, "How about you ride the boats instead?"

"No more rides, Daddy. They're too scary."

Behind her, he heard the rumbling of a car on a track, closely followed by the squeals of zealous riders. Looking up into the cloudy night, he watched the coaster glide along and disappear back into the rectangular building beneath it. The foreboding structure was just weather-worn plywood painted black, yet it held menace. Despite the cool night air, Charlie's forehead was covered in sweat. He could have let go of the fact that the ride was running. His responsibility had been met when he inspected it yesterday, yet he pulled his daughter toward the makeshift building.

The ride was operating when it shouldn't have been, and Charlie's instinct was to take his frustration out on the odd-looking man who ran the traveling amusement park but thought better of it when he remembered his large build covered with a collection of peculiar tattoos. Charlie took a deep breath, filling his lungs with the early October air mixed with the smell of popcorn and stale beer.

Dodging gawky teenagers and families who were oblivious to the sound pollution they were creating, he weaved along the un-even ground on his way to the ride. Each squeal of rambunctious carnival goers made him tense up. Cheap rides were something he'd never understood.

Passing a tent with a fading mural of a woman's face on a spi-der's body, he froze. The barker was chewing something wrapped in a dirty cloth that looked like an oversized fly. Her exposed hands were hairy, and she must have been wearing contact lenses, as her tiny eyes were glowing red. Looking at Charlie, she grinned, her lips creating a small, tight circle that seemed restricted by some unseen fo rce.

Swallowing hard, he, for the tenth time in the last few min-utes, wondered who in their right mind would come here to be purposefully frightened. The question was instantly followed by an evaluation of his own life. Why was he the only person qualified to inspect the rides? Considering his fear of the dark, heights, and rides in general, it didn't seem fair. Leaving such deep thoughts for more appropriate and quieter surroundings, he walked away, hoping the woman's face wasn't now indelibly imprinted into his mind to visit him when he was alone.

Dodging balloons, he made his way up the creaking back steps of the ride. As much as he wanted to, it wasn't in him to shirk his responsibility. Shirley was pulling back, feeling like an anchor. "Honey, come on."

"I'm not going to ride it, Daddy."

"Of course not. That's for big kids." *Who are insane.* "I just need to speak to the man running it for a minute."

"Are you a-trickin' me?" She dug in, her tiny feet planted into the mashed grass. "Of course not. Come on, honey."

She squeezed his fingers so hard that Charlie considered ignoring the carnival's infraction and leaving. When the ride reappeared, rolling along the track through two black doors, Shirley clutched his leg with her free hand. There was chanting from deep inside the rectangular building, barely audible over the laughing of the riders. After removing decades-old lap belts, the group left the ride, their faces full of life.

Reacting to so many happy people, Shirley loosened her grip. "All right, Daddy, I trust you."

Her words resonated deeply. Since the divorce, besides meeting his financial responsibilities, he was most concerned that she would never trust him again. Charlie was sure his ex constantly told his daughter all his faults. Although she was only four, he sensed disappointment in her.

He pulled Shirley along the landing; the thin plywood below bowed as he walked.

Bouncing along, the carnival manager, when seeing Charlie, quickly approached with his hand out.

"Good to see you again... sir."

He reeked of a funeral parlor—flowery—and of an indescribable disinfectant. Charlie reluctantly took the man's hand and was instantly rewarded with crushed fingers. The anger he was trying to ignore rose, making his face flush. "Although I didn't give you a permit, the ride is running now, Mr. Hill?" The man's eyes flashed just enough that Charlie knew whatever came next would be a lie.

"Well, yes." His mouth opened and quickly shut, as if he were biting off the next group of words. His sparse teeth poked through his chapped lips as he smiled. "As we discussed earlier, it's working."

"Yes, and as I stated, it needs to run *while* I inspect it to open it, hence why I did not give it a certificate. You know running it like this will cost you a hefty fine, right?"

"Sir, we travel coast to coast all year. Every other inspector has cleared it after they looked it over. No one else has such strict rules."

The line of people waiting to get on the ride seemed to call out in unison. The loudest voice yelled, "Hey, what's the hold-up?" Swaying back and forth like zombies, they leaned against the temporary ropes, staring with wanting, frightened eyes.

"Others' incompetence is neither my responsibility nor concern." Charlie looked at the aging cars on the dark track a foot below the loading platform. Everything around him was curved, and nothing like the other rides in the park. The equipment was dated in color and design like it came from the '50s. Every bit of its styling reminded him of a serpent. It was more than a slight curve. The cars looked as if they would slither along.

Following the length of the track that disappeared into double doors, he saw a very short man in the narrow opening. He quickly scurried away when spotted. Charlie squinted, thinking he saw a chain around his ankle. Even knowing it had to be some trick of the light, he still had the urge to run.

He said, "You need to cease operation immediately."

A vision of the shadow man grabbing Charlie and pulling him into the darkness appeared from deep in his brain. *They outnumber you, and nobody knows you're here. The ex thinks you're back at your place.* Shaking away the thought, sweat beaded stronger on his forehead despite the growing cold breeze.

Hill slicked back the last small patch of hair on his pointy head. "Yes, of course." He walked to a stand that looked like a podium and clicked on a few obscured buttons. His action apparently lit up something, making his face appear to glow momentarily, accentuating his deep wrinkles. In the darkness of the enclosed structure, the chanting grew louder.

Looking for speakers, Charlie took a step back, inspecting the face of the building and the track that jutted out in a loop above the housed area. It was skillfully painted, making it appear like a moving flame.

As he inspected every curve, the noise of what sounded like a hundred people inside was whispering in unison, "Stay away, stay far away. Before it gets you!" After a few seconds of quiet, there was a loud cackling, setting Charlie's nerves further on edge.

The voices rose and fell into a repeated chorus. Charlie pulled his daughter closer, asking Hill, "Is that... coming from inside the ride?"

"Yes." Hill's eyes darted to the cars, and then, as if viewing something repulsive, he went back to the operator's podium with a pained look.

"Charming." The vision of the doors opening and swallowing him came back. *Better get out of here, buddy, and fast.*

"The Demon is a rite of passage for our younger... guests. It's their chance to prove their bravery. The soundtrack enhances that experience."

Charlie thought of his daughter, hoping she would never feel pressured to expose herself to such childish antics. A good portion of his youth had been spent avoiding such nonsense as terrorizing yourself in the name of bravery.

The manager pulled a lever, and the ride moaned as the cars edged forward a few inches.

Charlie felt the vibration beneath him as the drive chain creaked.

Multiple voices from the crowd cheered, pushing forward. The retaining ropes were stretched to their limit. Their momentum seemed to mix with the air energizing it.

Hill smiled at them. "Would you care to ride it? You've already inspected the interior.

Won't that prove it's operational?"

"Daddy! You're tricking me!"

Shirley's fingers were like vise grips digging into his leg. "No, I wouldn't like to ride it!"

Remember the first and last time you rode a roller coaster? Fighting to remain in control over the man he had no respect for, Charlie quickly added, "I meant, no, that isn't necessary." He pushed his daughter behind him, saying, "It's all right. I promise you don't ever have to ride it."

"Please understand, Inspector, I *need* the ride running tonight. Can't you just take a quick ride?" The man massaged the back of his neck. The tattoos on his forearm danced along his sagging skin with the movement. "For your time, I will give you an unlimited pass on all our rides and games."

Shirley poked her head out from behind Charlie. "Then we could win Mr. Cutey Bear!" Her voice seemed to frighten her. Quickly, she returned to her hiding spot, burying her face against his pants.

Hill bent forward. "Yes, little one. I can arrange for you to have a choice of any prize." Seeing the man's eyes on his daughter made Charlie's stomach turn.

"Keep your tickets. I'm not working this evening. And even if I did inspect it, it wouldn't save you the fine."

"Please, I'll pay the fine. I just need the ride running tonight."

"Please, Daddy. I need my bear."

Thinking of all the times he had let her down this past year after the divorce, he stood up straight and sighed deeply. "I would need to go inside and inspect the motor."

The words made his stomachache worse, but he knew he had to face the fear or feel like a coward to the last person in the world who thought he was still capable of being brave.

"But you already did!"

"Yes, but it was idle then. It's necessary to look it over while the ride is moving."

"I don't see the point, sir." The false smile disappeared, giving way to the gruff face Charlie had seen earlier in the day. In a brief flash, his expression told the many hardships of the carnival worker's life.

"Okay, then. Let me put it to you this way. If you run this again tonight without me inspecting, and without getting a certificate from the town of New Bremen, we will contact the next ten towns you're going to and be sure they don't allow you adequate permits to open."

"You don't understand!" Hill rubbed his mouth with the back of his hand, exposing filthy palms. With his tongue working over a gap where his front tooth should be, he finally said, "Okay. Okay, if you must. I'll let you inside. Just give me a minute."

The carnival manager walked up to a gawky teenager, who resembled a miniature version of him, whispering into the boy's ear. The younger man put up a rope, holding back the rest of the lines. There was a collective groan, and someone threw a box of popcorn that scattered over the platform. The snack looked like snowflakes across the dirty ground.

Hill spoke into a walkie-talkie and then walked back to Charlie. "Can you please make this quick? As you can see, we have many people waiting."

"I won't be rushed." Charlie peered through the shadows of the double doors. The voices resumed again. This time, they sounded like different people entirely. Bending down, he said,

"Pumpkin, you're going to help me do some work, then we'll go and win you your bear. Okay?"

"We gotta go into there?" She drew her head back—the slight effort dislodging her hair from the rubber band.

"Yes. Just for a few minutes."

She shook her head wildly, her bangs covering her eyes. Her mouth opened, but no words came out.

"If you want to leave, we can," Charlie willed her to say yes. It would let him out of his ultimatum, so he could avoid going into the dark space.

She looked down, making circles in the dust with her worn shoes, which she was quickly growing out of. "It's okay, Daddy. I can be brave." She swiped the hair out of her face. "I know I can do it for Mr. Cutey Bear."

He was up against it now. "All right, then."

Hill eagerly hit a button on the podium. The doors creaked open, letting the smell of oil and dust mix with the night air. He stepped down, walking sideways on a narrow platform running parallel to the ride.

"Watch your step." There was no longer any pretense of kindness in his voice. His eyes were daggers, staring through his unwelcome guest as he looked back.

Charlie followed along, pulling Shirley carefully and avoiding the rails. He knew it wasn't powered with an open current but felt that if he touched it, the cool metal would harm them irreparably. The surrounding curved walls that drew closer as he went forward were a string of blinking multicolored bulbs, disorienting him.

Shielding his eyes with his free hand, he called out, "Can you turn those off!" Hill pulled out a walkie-talkie. "Owen, cut the show lights."

There was a metallic clang, and complete darkness enveloped them. Time seemed to stop in the belly of the ride.

The carny pulled out a flashlight, its beam catching the curved walls. Pointing with his head, he said, "The door's just around the corner."

Fighting to keep the bubbling anxiety out of his voice, he grated, "Yeah, I remember." The chanting came back on, vibrating and pulsating. Charlie cringed, the cryptic words enveloping him. The deep bass seemed to work through his skin to his bones. "You all right, Pumpkin?"

"Uh-huh."

"We can go back if you are scared."

"Nope. I'm okay, Daddy." She gave a gap-toothed smile, displaying the newest void that had gone to the tooth fairy.

Hill pulled an overflowing keychain from his belt. Fumbling with the handle, he opened the door to the machine's motor room. A single bulb on a wooden ceiling illuminated pulleys, chains, and belts wrapped around a great motor that seemed to go on endlessly in the tight area.

Lifting his daughter over the track, Charlie stepped past him, wondering how they transported something so intricate and bulky. A phantom echo clanged in the distance.

"See, boss? Nothing's changed."

He put Shirley down, forcing a smile, not wanting her to see who her father really was.

Turning, he tucked his shirt in. "Regardless, we have rules for a reason, Hill."

Charlie's eyes traced the engine, not knowing what half the valves did. Everything was so old that it looked like it predated the First World War. "Please have your people start the ride, and we can finish this up."

The walkie-talkie came out again. "Start her up, Owen."

"Stay away, stay far away."

The bass from the speakers made Charlie's fillings hurt. "Please turn that off!"

"Can't. It's on the same circuit as the cars. To run the ride, the soundtrack goes, Inspector."

There was vibrating, followed by the creaking of chains. Shirley clutched Charlie's arm. He put his hand on top of her head. "Almost done, little one." The words were swallowed up in the chanting.

A large wheel spun just in front of Charlie, creaking and pulling what looked like a giant rubber band that appeared like it would snap at any time. Taking a small step back, Shirley moved as far away as possible. He felt the whoosh of the car passing the room from the right.

Get out of here before it's too late!

The blinking lights came back on, cascading shadows across the walls, making him dizzy.

Charlie put his hand against the machine to regain his balance. Hot metal seared his skin. He pulled back and bit his pinky finger to cool it. The voices came from every direction, causing Charlie to jump and pull his arms in as if he were protecting himself from a blow.

The carny smiled. "Seen enough, Inspector?"

Needing to feel in control, he responded sharply, "Not quite! Still need to check the coolant." The words seemed to come from someone else.

Why are you still here? Get out!

On wobbly legs, disentangling himself from Shirley, he stepped to the left of the engine, letting go of his daughter's hand. Seeing a large tube housing multiple wires, he stopped.

Knowing what he was seeing couldn't be made him quiver.

"Hill!" Charlie's eyes moved around the tight space. The raging engine picked up steam, shooting noises in multiple directions. "Where's the power source?"

The thick electrical cord coming from the belly of the motor was a jumble of loose wires lying on the dirt floor, not connected to anything.

The sound of a chain being dragged very near was behind him. He turned quickly, and pain exploded across the back of his head. Thinking his eyes would pop out of their sockets, Charlie raised his hands to hold them in as everything went black.

Opening his eyes took effort, revealing blurriness surrounded by a dull light. There was a loud humming noise and a faint scream in the distance. Charlie didn't know where he was, or where he'd been, but he sensed something tragic would happen if he didn't sit up.

The few inches he crept forward made the back of his head ache so badly that he could taste burning acid on his tongue. Realizing it was vomit, he turned, covering his mouth and holding it in. The slight movement brought a pounding in his skull.

"Take it easssy."

The voice sounded like that of an actor imitating a serpent. Wiping his eyes with the back of his hand, Charlie squinted and could make out red glowing eyes a few feet from him.

"Pleassse, sssir, relaxxx."

He remembered a cartoon once where a snake charmer coaxed a viper out of a wicker box when reality struck. *Where's Shirley?* Her memory came as an odor. He smelled on his sleeve the cheap laundry detergent that his ex insisted he use, and the terror ejected the bile he'd just swallowed.

"There, there now, sssir. It'll all be fine."

Coughing felt like fire on the back of his throat. "Where's my daughter!" His scream brought a sharp, throbbing pain across the right side of his face.

"You've had an accccident."

"Where is she!" Closing his eyes, he forced himself into a sitting position. His head felt like it was four times its regular size. Gripping the ground, his neck strained, making his torso shake.

"Ssshe's fine. Sssshe's with Mr. Hill."

Imagining the man's tattooed arms wrapped around Shirley, he yelped, "Bring her to me now!"

"In due time."

He tried to stand, and blackness floated at the edges of his vision. Letting out a deep breath, he was back on the ground. "Please, help me get to her."

"There'sss no reason to be upset, sssir. We've ssssent for medical help."

Charlie closed his left eye and could just make out the spider lady. She was working her hands over, caressing them frantically. His eyes traced her ridiculously tight costume. Her feet were exposed and hairy, appearing not to have any toes. The area around her ankle was matted, as if a clamp had recently been removed. Hoping it was a costume, he realized her odd voice was possibly just an ordinary lisp and not a result of her being part-insect like his imagination was trying to get him to believe.

The thought did little to quiet his nerves. "When?"

"They'll be here sssoon."

You're never getting out of here. Noise was coming from above, and he quickly recognized the muffled sound as the chanting of the ride. "What struck my head?" He slowly raised his hand. The back of his head was moist and felt like Jell-O.

"I couldn't sssay. I wasssn't there, sssir."

"Can you call Mr. Hill? I need my daughter, now." The room seemed to be growing smaller, trying to swallow him up.

"He's on the ride with her."

"What... *why?*" Charlie opened both eyes, instantly regretting it. It brought a pain like a thin hot wire inserted through his eye socket to the back of his skull.

"To feed the ride." She reached out, caressing the wall with her hairy hand.

"What does that *mean?*" It felt like his blood was turning solid, coursing through his veins, about to burst through his skin.

"This ride livesss on fear, ssssir. When the young ones are willing to ride and go through the dark passssage, it feeds off that fear. It's what keeps it alive." She looked up at the ceiling, trying to smile but not quite making it. "Don't worry; it won't harm your girl. In fact, it will make her real ssstrong. Once the fear isss out, the ride devoursss it as they russsh through the dark tunnel."

What is she saying? From somewhere above, there was the sound of a great vibrating coaster rattling the entire structure. The shrieks from the riders went through Charlie, making him weaker. *"Why?"*

"Thisss ride hasss traveled the country sssince well before mosssst of ussss were born.

All we know is to feed it, or it will take far more than jussst fear, sssir."

"Look! I don't care about your foolish story! I work for the county. Do you understand? I demand you bring me my daughter!"

The woman's expression didn't change. She stared at him with the disinterest of a church patron.

Charlie desperately added, "If you do, I'll leave and approve the ride to keep running, no questions asked. I promise."

Stay away, stay far away. Before it gets you! The chanting grew louder. Charlie's eyes searched shadows, expecting to see a group of wild demons advancing upon him.

"Please, please help me up! I need to get out of here, now!"

The spider woman stood up from a small stool, slowly advancing. "It'll all be over sssoon."

The door behind her opened, letting in erratic lights from the tunnel. Raising his hand to shield his eyes, Charlie watched Hill's shadow fill the doorway.

"He's awake. Very good."

Shirley was behind him as he stepped in, clutching his hand. Charlie, despite the pain, grunted and stood. The dirt below him felt as if it were shifting.

"Sir, please sit down. A doctor will be here very soon."

His head pulsated. When he closed his left eye, he could almost see clearly with the right. "Shirley, come here."

She looked up at Hill, smiling. "Okay, Daddy." She walked toward Charlie, looking happier than he'd ever seen her. Her remaining whiskers on her cheeks danced as she smiled.

The warmth from her hand gave Charlie strength. Clutching her, he took a tentative step forward. He was woozy but felt almost strong enough to move on.

"Sir, please, you aren't well!"

"Out of my way." The man didn't budge. Not up to any physical confrontation, he said, "I give you my word, if you let us pass, I won't tell anyone that you struck me as you did."

"What? I didn't hit you. You passed out. You said something about power, then passed out and hit your head on the motor."

"Fine. Tell yourself that. Just let us leave."

"I can prove it. Please come into the engine room. You can see where you struck the motor." His wild eyes grew larger as he pointed to the dark doorway. "There's still blood on it."

"Good, take me th—" *Do you really want proof that this machine is running on fear?* Charlie couldn't move. *It's better to leave and never look back.* Each breath stung deep in his lungs. He looked down at Shirley; she was grinning ear to ear. Every muscle tensed as he tried to take a small step forward. "I'm leaving now. Just stay out of my way."

The man held both of his hands up in a resigned motion. "Whatever you say, Inspector. Don't say I didn't warn you."

As he passed Hill, he whispered to Charlie, "If you tell anyone what happened here, you will regret it."

Charlie dragged Shirley into the dark hallway, nearly suffocating on the musty smell. The enclosed area looked as if it hadn't seen daylight in decades. His head was pounding, making everything move at twice the speed it should. Clutching the loose railing, he concentrated on each step.

Up the stairway, he saw the side exit he'd entered earlier that day.

"Daddy, are you okay? You look kinda funny."

"I'll be fine." *How about you, dear? Did the ride gobble up your fear? Feel better now?* Charlie gripped the makeshift railing, willing the dark thoughts away. "We've just got to get out of here, Pumpkin."

The chanting vibrated through him. *Stay away, stay far away!*

Moving faster than he should, he pushed the door open and was instantly assaulted by the night air. The kinetic movement of the carnival added to Charlie's disorientation. He couldn't believe there were still smiling people in the world.

Finally, at a safe distance away, back in the main thoroughfare and surrounded by screaming throngs of people, Charlie looked back. The shrieks of the riders hurt his insides. He knew it would be best to turn back and confront the fear rather than carry it with him forever, but he knew he couldn't.

Bending down, he asked the question he didn't want an answer to. "What'd you do with that man? Did he take you on the ride?"

"I'm not supposed to talk about that." She looked to the ground, staring at her tiny feet.

"Honey, are you okay? Did he do..." He bit off the last words, knowing he couldn't cope with the answer. Not now, not here.

"I'm happy, Daddy."

She wiped his tears. Her tiny hand ran against his beard stubble. He patted her head, moving back strands of hair. The contact melted his heart. "You're sure? No one hurt you?"

"Oh, no, we had fun once the scary part was over."

He looked past her back to the Demon. He could see the fear on the faces of the riders going through the loop. The coaster moved so fast that it distorted them, making it appear like a vapor was coming off the riders. *That's the fear the Demon's gonna eat. Why don't you go back and be free of it once and for all?* Charlie turned away, pulling Shirley along.

Tugging, she insisted, "Daddy, I want my bear."

"I'm sorry. Not tonight, Pumpkin." *Nor any other night, coward.*

The faint screams behind him were constant reminders of how much things had changed this long night—each noise taunting him. He glanced back once more at the enormous loop.

What if it takes more than just fear?

Charlie, knowing his next step would define him, pulled Shirley closer. Defeated, he made his way out of the carnival, going back to his ordinary life.

TENDENCIES

Being as close to death as many times as I have, at least indirectly, I'm pretty surprised that I've never really questioned what happens after someone's time is up. I guess this all started in the audio-visual club during my first year of high school. Those were the days long before therapists, shrinks, and counselors would use terms like "sociopathic tendencies" and other descriptions that I had to look up. Back then, I was always better with equipment than words or people, for that matter. That was before I developed my gift of "gab," as my grandma used to call it. She was a mean old bat, but she was always good with quips like that.

Anyway, I taught myself how to fix pretty much anything that had a tube or speakers when I was pretty young. Saying I taught myself is a bit of a lie, but you'll understand soon enough. The first time I discovered my special ability was when I was messing with Bill Humphrey's transistor radio when I was only eight. He had been by to make out with my sister for their regular Wednesday night romp. They were afforded an empty house, except for me, thanks to my parents' weekly date night. As usual, when my sister's overgrown suitor arrived, they went straight upstairs. Every time, right after he got there, Harriet warned me that she would beat me within an inch of my life if I followed them. My sister, although having a very pretty face, was no small girl, so I always took those warnings seriously.

On that night, Bill left his leather jacket—he really had no business calling it leather anymore; it had more cloth patches than leather, yet he carried on like it was made of gold—on top of my chair fort, crushing the sheet I used as a canopy. Pissed—not a word an eight-year-old would use, I know—I grabbed the stinking patchwork, trying to reassemble my makeshift teepee, and his handheld radio slipped from the pocket, nearly landing square on my bare toes. Always agile, I hopped away at the last second, leaving it to fall on the floor. The faceplate with the station numbers went shooting into the baseboard, leaving the carcass behind to bleed wire guts. Knowing I was going to get it if they heard anything, I grabbed the pieces and ducked into the deformed fort.

As I sat there holding my breath and listening for footsteps on the old wooden stairs, I had what believers might call an epiphany. In my stubby, filthy fingers, I could feel the radio talking to me. It wasn't like you would think; it didn't use words. It vibrated. Each pulse ran up my arms, and somehow, my flesh gave the vibrations words. Not the sort of words I was used to hearing. Instead, it communicated with pictures in my head. As I sat there, I felt vibrations through my entire body and saw images playing like a TV show.

Step by step, I watched myself putting the radio back together. I didn't float around like a ghost; it was more like there was a camera inside my skull, taping. I could see my arms, body, and hands working, but not my face. It was weird because the images came while my eyes were open, so the radio surgery was happening over everything else I could see. After it stopped, I went into the tool drawer in my parent's kitchen and, within minutes, had the plastic radio back together.

Telling the story now, I can only guess that anybody would have a hard time understanding how easy it was for me to accept what had happened. But at the time, my eight-year-old mind thought nothing of the event. It seemed perfectly normal that this knowledge would be made available like that. Anyway, feeling like I'd dodged a solid beating, I put the radio back in the jacket, and as painful as it was, I put it back on top of my beautiful fort, crushing i t.

A week later, it was date night again. Harriet had over a new beau whom I'd never seen before. He was a scrawny dude with slicked-back hair. After the prerequisite beating threat, I was alone once again, sitting under the kitchen table. At that age, I had a thing for hiding places.

As I sat there, the vibration I'd felt from the radio was back like a tiny electric current running through my veins. It wasn't a bad feeling, but it wasn't good, either. It was just a solid feeling, kind of like when you're in the shower, waiting for the temperature to get just right.

Anyway, a few seconds later, I heard music as if I were wearing headphones, and then suddenly, I could see inside Bill Humphrey's car. I didn't know it was his car right away because, at first, I only saw two people hugging together in the back seat. Suddenly, large hairy fingers almost completely obscured my view.

As they rolled the dial, I heard new wave music coming through the single car speaker. Looking across my living room, I saw the new image kind of floating in the air over my dad's bookcase, which was filled with the spaceship models that he was so obsessed with.

When Bill backed off, I saw a girl who was much shapelier than Harriet in the right kind of way. That explained the new scrawny creep upstairs.

For the next few minutes, I watched Bill try to romance the pretty girl. That was a joke.

He would have been better off sticking with his normal Wednesday thing, even if my sister wasn't in that girl's class.

Again, I know there will be doubters out there who won't believe that I didn't freak out, but honestly, maybe it shows my stupidity, but I thought nothing of it. If I'm forced to explain it—and a-hole shrinks have asked me more times than I can count—it was because I didn't have anyone who gave a damn.

My parents weren't bad people. They never beat us too badly or deprived us of anything reasonable. Many have told me that not giving love to a child is abuse. The way I look at it, I couldn't yearn for something that I didn't know existed.

Whenever I said that to any therapist, the notepad always came out, and a flourish of notes went down. In those moments, I imagined what they had written. My usual guess was *this one is a Freudian mess. No love. How could he ever get through that?* But honestly, I wasn't that bad off, regardless of what the head doctors wanted to say. There were many worse people who could have raised us.

As I learned in the coming months, the connection to the radio was not temporary. Every Wednesday night at eight, if the radio was on—it took me far too long to figure that part out—I could see what was in front of it. The viewings became part of my life, the same as going to school or cutting the lawn. I didn't particularly look forward to them because I never knew what I would stare at and believe me, watching Bill dancing and lip-synching in the bathroom in only his underwear was no treat.

The next "viewing moment" came when I was ten. By chance, my parents came across a used Atari console for a couple of bucks and gave it to me for my birthday. That summer, I used up my entire allowance buying away Harriet's TV time. That was before I learned I could blackmail her with how she really spent my parents' date nights.

Anyway, on a rainy Saturday at precisely 4:02 p.m., the old cathode tube gave out, just as I was completing Level Eight of *Monster Dodgers*. Yes, Level Eight! That one had taken me a week to memorize.

Devastated, I stared at my reflection on the glass tube, wanting to cry—not just over level eight, but because I knew there was likely no budget for a new TV anytime soon.

Finally, it came to me to reach out and place my palm on the screen. Then, it happened exactly the same as it had with Bill's transistor. The vibration began, and I viewed the repair. However, the hope that it brought quickly became anguish because the repair would require a soldering iron, and the most complex tool in my dad's arsenal was a multi-tool that came as a free gift with a wine and cheese wheel.

I tried to come up with a scheme to scam back my allowance money when it came to me.

Mr. Crane would have a soldering tool. He had to. The guy had everything, and I mean *everything*. One Sunday, I'd seen him in his garage with a blowtorch. Now, if I told him it was for my dad, I knew it would be a definite no, but if I could get him to believe that we had a repairman over, there was a slight chance. Luckily for me, the old man wasn't home, and Mrs. Crane gave me what I needed.

Back at my house, I followed the instructions I'd just viewed and had the TV working in less than half an hour.

The next Saturday, I had two regularly scheduled programs on my private viewing network. Unfortunately, the TV never showed me anything of interest, but it's disorienting to watch yourself play a video game.

It wasn't until late into my freshman year that I started learning how to use my viewing moments to my advantage. I guess I was a late bloomer because while all the kids I hung around with were chasing after girls, I was still playing video games or reading comics until I met Mary Louise.

She was a freshman just like me, and really, I never noticed her until the day she wore that white blouse that April. Our desks were jammed way too close in those old rooms, so I would have to lean sideways to see the board, too timid to ask her to move over.

That all changed the day she walked in, wearing the thin fabric over her lacy bra. I could see every detail, front and back, as if she were topless. I didn't learn much in class that day, other than what it felt like to be lovesick. For the entire period, I did nothing but sit mesmerized by Mary Louise.

That was the first time the thought occurred to me that I could use my "gift" to my advantage. I didn't have an exact plan, but my mind ran with hundreds of possibilities, all ending with seeing that bra. Whatever she'd done to me was infectious, because after the dismissal bell, I saw the girls in my school in a completely different way.

My newfound appreciation turned to Mrs. Vagle, the French teacher, who put Mary Louise's underthings to shame. Remembering she had a TV in her classroom—the standard twenty-inch kind bolted to a wheeled cart—inspiration finally struck.

The next morning, I did something I wasn't especially proud of. Unsure if it would work, I sneaked into her class fifteen minutes before she arrived and busted her TV.

Less than a minute after I yanked the circuit board, the vision began. It felt like cheating, considering that I was the one who had caused it, but either way, the picture movie showed me how to reconnect what I'd just undone.

A week later, as I sat in algebra, I had the pleasure of viewing Vagle from clear across the school. For the entire period, I got to watch the room and, fortunately, the goddess who instructed the class never disappointed.

By that time, I was figuring out how all of this worked. Whenever I fixed something, a week later, I could see through it. It was the same as the transistor—if the device was on, I saw what it saw.

It was already late in the year, but I met with Mr. Spencer, who ran the AV club. He explained that he would let me join, but because of my late start, I wouldn't have the privileges the other kids had, like being in the yearbook photo. I nodded, playing the game, thinking the whole time, *Like I give a shit, those kids don't like me anyway.* All I wanted was to find a way into the girls' locker room.

The AV group met every Tuesday and Thursday after school, divvying up the to-do list, making sure that teachers' requests were met, and maintaining the equipment. For obvious reasons, I quickly became one of the top technicians. Not only did I tune up the simple stuff, like erasing squiggly lines on the videotapes, but I also resurrected, as Mr. Spencer said, several of the TVs that had been out of circulation for a while.

I would like to say that I learned a lot during that time, but really, it was just simple memorization. The instructions hung in my head until I completed the task. It was like walking into a test with a cheat sheet. The other guys in the group were a timid bunch—go figure—so they didn't push back too hard when I refused to do anything after school. If I fixed it, it had to be during school hours. I did my best to stagger the times. If they overlapped, I would get two viewings at the same time. Let me tell you: until you get used to it, you get nauseous seeing so much, and that's not a lot of fun.

By the end of that semester, my list of viewing materials had grown to a point where I only had free hours at night. It certainly helped me get through the boredom of my class load. The distraction tanked my grades, but by then, I'd mastered my parents' signatures, so as long as I passed, it wasn't an issue.

My parents were always open to being lied to. When they asked how school was, I could make up whatever I felt like, and they ate it up without so much as a single question.

Everything was going well until the day Mr. Grundy put in the request for the TV/VCR combo to be brought into his room. That was the day I learned that greed was, indeed, bad. It's useless to look back, but I still do it all the time.

Grundy was the prototypical a-hole teacher who got off on making the semester as hard as he could for his students. His specialty was calculus, and his final exam was legendary. Most kids spent a week studying for it, and for their efforts, they were happy with a D.

During my fourth-period world history class, right before lunch, my viewing was of an empty room. Normally, this would upset me. At this point, I'd become an addict for having, at minimum, two things going, but the TV was facing Grundy's desk. Sitting in plain view on top of the desk was the answer grid for the final. It was the old multiple-choice circle sheet that required a No. 2 pencil. An opportunity not to be missed: I copied the answers into my notebook.

As a freshman, I knew only one senior, Lenny Meratti, and it was because our dads worked in the same office, keeping an inventory of auto parts. I hunted him down after school, remembered his locker was in the north wing, and made the proposition. Twenty bucks for the answers.

He was a beefy guy—not all fat, just overall, larger than everyone else, which helped him play for the football team and intimidate me. Pulling me into the locker room, he made me guarantee that the answers were legit before trying to negotiate the price down. With him hovering over me and with both arms pressing me against the wall, I convinced him that the cheat sheet was legit by offering him all my game cartridges if I was wrong. It did the trick. We settled on $15, and I gave him the answers.

Well, the overgrown goon had a bigger mouth than I had expected. By the weekend, half the football team had a copy of the test, and wouldn't you know it, Brandon, the quarterback—aren't those guys supposed to be the smart ones—got pinched with it. Worried that it would hurt his scholarship, the shithead squealed on Lenny.

I didn't get that information from a viewing moment. Oddly enough, Mary Louise, wearing a cream top with a fantastic black bra beneath, told Doug Linderman in health class while I viewed kids' reactions to an instructional video on the female reproductive system. It wasn't easy to ignore that one, as it was choice viewing, but when I heard about someone getting nabbed with all the answers to Grundy's test, it certainly got my attention.

Knowing that I had to get to Lenny, I counted down the last ten minutes of class, feeling like they were measured in dog years. I caught him in the hall heading to his locker and got him to follow me to the locker room. He laughed when I begged him not to turn me in, and it was the first time I realized killing meant nothing to me. I wasn't angry or passionate. I was just there, watching the jowls of his neck shake as he laughed. As he did, I decided there was only one way to stop him—that was when I pulled the penknife from my pocket and jabbed it right into his fat neck. That shut him up real quick.

I'd seen enough TV to somewhat anticipate the blood that would shoot from the wound, but let me tell you, it gushed out like a river. Always agile, I jumped onto the bench that separated the lockers and watched the stream squirt across the room.

The fat idiot fell to his knees, choking on the blood that didn't paint the walls. While I watched him die, it occurred to me that it was like watching one of my viewings. Like his pain was on display, simply for my amusement. Confident he was done, I washed the knife and my hands in the stainless steel sink that everyone shared and then walked out of the locker room to lunch. Burritos was on offer. I never felt great about eating them after hearing the rumor about someone finding a Band-Aid in one. Halfway through lunch, I heard the squad car pull up.

Munching thoughtfully to make sure it was only burrito material I was chewing, I watched the teachers gather.

A few minutes later, Mr. Swenson stood on the stage of the shared auditorium that the goofy-ass school made us eat in. He called for everyone's attention and said that no one could leave the room, as there had been an accident. I wondered if he knew what really had happened or if he was just trying to keep everyone calm.

That was the day I learned how easy it was to kill someone and get away with it. School was closed for the rest of the week, making for some boring viewings, which made me dread summer. What if someone was dumb enough to leave their TV on all summer? I'd never thought it through, but I could've been close to being stuck looking at dull, empty classrooms.

What I did learn was that cheating didn't pay off. I didn't care that Lenny was dead. I probably saved his future wife from a lifetime of abuse, but I did realize that I could have been caught. Later, I found out that Coach Mester had been in his office, four rows of lockers away from... That's how close it had been. Who knows what would have happened if that old shit hadn't been sneaking in a nap or whatever he'd been doing? That worried me to the point that I promised myself that next time, I would be a lot more careful.

———

The remainder of high school was more of the same. Not killing; I took some time off from that, but my viewing calendar kept expanding. My seven-period day was filled, and I even had four overlaps in there.

My nights were fairly open, except for the transistor. Bill eventually left it in a box in his attic, so that was a tough hour until the batteries drained because the moron had left the power on.

The only other night-viewing was Harriet's Walkman. I should have known better, and I did, but I thought I might catch a glimpse of Barbara, Harriet's buxom best friend, when they did dance aerobics together. So, I fixed the tape-playing machine after she sat on it. If I'd known that Harriet sometimes kept it in her bra when she went walking, I would have bought her a new one and saved myself a lot of trauma. As I watched those enormous sweaty melons swinging, the hardest part was that I could still see the awful broadcast, even when I closed my eyes. That was when I learned that, although I could receive transmissions, I had no control over the connection.

As I said before, you get addicted to other people's lives pretty quickly, so I had to find a way to fill my nights. It had gotten to the point that I got anxious when I saw reality in front of me. That prompted me to look for a way to increase the frequency between five and midnight.

This was what brought me to the video store—the first real job I ever had. I was hired as a clerk at Galaxy Video, and within a week, I had access to the rental VCRs.

It was perfect. My main job was hunting down movies for the customers. This was a small operation that had tags beneath the cardboard artwork instead of the actual VHS tapes, which were stored in the backroom behind the counter. Whenever it got slow, I would sit in the back and tune up the rental machines, whether they needed it or not. Within two weeks, I had a full-night schedule going.

I learned a lot about people at night. One of the biggest things I learned was how perverted they were. Half of what I saw at night was weirdos watching porno flicks and enjoying themselves. It was a lot of fun when it was couples imitating what they watched, but there were far more guys jerking off alone. If I'd thought watching Harriet was bad, it was nothing compared to watching some hairy-ass a-hole go to town on himself.

I really thought I'd learned something about cheating with the Lenny event, but I guess I was a slow learner. Of all the people to have a pervert in their family, I was shocked to find out that Mary Louise's dad had a peculiar fetish. It was during my Thursday 10:00 p.m. viewing that I got to watch the dentist jack himself off with a plastic bag over his head while watching one of Galaxy Video's nastier pornos. Some of the stuff that came out of the back room with the beads over the door was downright disgusting. None of the teenagers who worked there were allowed to check them out, but we would when no one was looking. I have never been one to judge others, but if you need to watch that kind of stuff to climax, you probably need some help.

Unfortunately for Mary Louise, her dad was one of them. I didn't have a choice, but it was mesmerizing to watch him get started, and then a minute in, place a plastic bag over his head and start sucking on the clear plastic until he passed out. The guy must have been some sort of jack-off genius to time it out like he did and to know that he was going to wake up. Then again, maybe that was the rush—thinking that maybe you wouldn't.

It really wasn't my thing, so I didn't spend a lot of time thinking about it. The whole deal lasted less than ten minutes, and my own TV was occupied by my dad watching some boring-ass documentary, so I was stuck looking at the balding naked dude with his shorts dangling around his legs, sleeping off the jizz high he was on with my dad next to him.

As I looked around the room to avoid him, I saw something that interested me. Next to the bed was a small makeup table. I kind of hoped it belonged to the dentist's wife and wasn't another fetish. On the table sat a huge magnifying mirror. In the reflection, I saw a dresser and a wall safe.

The safe should have been hidden behind a painting. There was a dirty outline on the wallpaper where the painting should have been hanging. On the safe was a Post-it note with a series of numbers in scribbled ink.

Jackpot!

That night, I went back and forth a couple hundred times, trying to decide how much could possibly be in the safe. I told myself I was just daydreaming, but to be honest, I knew I would find a way to get in there and clean it out.

The next morning, before leaving for school, I found their address in the phonebook. If I went a half mile in the wrong direction, I discovered I could check it out on my walk to school.

A week went by before I was confident that I could get in and out with relative ease. Mary Louise was an only child, and her mother worked as a hygienist at her father's office. Calling from a payphone, I disguised my voice and tried to make a dental appointment for Friday after school. Both had other patients but could see me the next week on Tuesday.

I knew Mary Louise was in band, and Friday was homecoming, so she would be out of the way as well. This was no longer a what-if. I had to know what was in that safe. That only left one obstacle: Could I fit in the doggy door? They had a cocker spaniel, but the vinyl flap was twice the size it had to be. From what I could see from their neighbor's yard, they had an old shed I could hide behind, and I felt confident that I could contort myself through.

I was eager to get going that afternoon but chose to wait until four-thirty because there was a more distracting viewing at four. It was the AV TV that was now in the teachers' lounge, and on Fridays, the alcohol came out to welcome the weekend. I expected the rented VCR to be blacked out by four-thirty. Everything worked perfectly.

As it turned out, I was right. There was no viewing. I could have managed it if there were, but it was better this way.

My first obstacle was nothing. The doggy door took no effort. With almost no pressure, I slipped right through. The cocker spaniel was asleep. As I tiptoed past, for a brief second, it looked up at me and then went right back to its nap.

I had memorized the combination, but I had a copy in my jeans pocket as backup. With a few turns, the door opened, and inside, sitting next to a few papers, were several necklaces and a pile of cash. I didn't know it at the time, but it was slightly under ten grand. I know it's not that much all in all, but it was a real score for a teenager in the early nineties.

I left the jewelry—I had no clue how to sell something like that—and made my way down the stairs. If it weren't for the motherfucking reed for the saxophone, everything would have gone down perfectly.

I must have been half-deaf or impaired by adrenaline because I did not hear Mary Louise walking up the stairs. She wore a tan dicky with a white bra underneath; it was made to go beneath her band jacket.

I rounded the corner, my backpack filled with the perverted dentist's loot, and almost knocked her over. She had an almost amused look on her face as she asked, "Aren't you the guy from my algebra class?"

I remember being surprised that she didn't scream or ask what I was doing there. That was the last emotion I felt as I grabbed the hunting knife, which I'd upgraded from the penknife in case I needed it for the dog, and plunged it into her eye socket.

I didn't do it to be gruesome. To be honest, I was planning on jamming it into her chest and totally whiffed. Before she could scream, I spun her around and had my hand over her mouth. My only thought was wondering if she liked the oxygen deprivation, like her father. She didn't struggle much; she just kind of twitched in a half-assed way. I was surprised that I didn't think of her in a sexual way. I could have done whatever I wanted, but the moment we shared was more important than that.

There was blood, but less than I thought there would be. I was wearing gloves, so I wasn't overly concerned, but then I noticed the darkened portion of my army jacket with the stencil of the Violent Femmes on the back.

I was pissed. That patch was hard to come by. I knew I would have to toss it, but I really didn't want to. I left the same way I came, frustrated not only by needing to ditch my jacket before I got back but also by the reed. If she hadn't forgotten it, she still would have been alive, and I would still get to enjoy watching her in her AP class at my two o'clock viewing. That lazy- ass teacher did little but play videos.

The money came in handy, even though I could only use small portions of it at a time. I kept it buried between the pages of my comic book collection, knowing it would be safe there. The last time anyone but me was in my bedroom was when I had a nasty flu in the sixth grade.

I kept my job at the video store, even though I didn't need the pay. It gave me the potential for unlimited viewings, which was good, even if I was tired of listening to the other clerks gabbing all day. I never quite understood their need to share every bit of bullshit that went through their heads, but they sure as hell thought they might explode if they didn't get it all out.

By the time high school was over, I had a pretty good schedule going that ran morning to night. I even experimented during my sleeping hours. I was hesitant at first but tried it for the shit of it, figuring I could always destroy the camera at the Stop & Save gas station if it kept me up too late.

I learned a pretty neat thing with that experiment. I could ignore it if the viewing started when I was asleep, which was great because then there was no risk.

I didn't kill again until I was twenty. I'm not going to lie; it surprised me. Mary Louise introduced me to bloodlust in the same way she had sexual lust. When I say that, I know it makes me sound like a maniac, but it really isn't like that at all. I've relived that moment in the hallway with her a thousand times. If I'm being honest, and at this point, there is no reason not to; everything I do now is geared toward trying to relive that exact experience, and that's why I keep stabbing them in the eye.

It isn't like the reporters say. It isn't because I see myself in the victims, or better yet, that I don't want them to see me because I feel shame. It's simply because her hallway was dark, and the angle wasn't quite what I thought it was. The a-hole shrinks finally have me convinced that I probably don't understand love, but that moment with her is probably the closest I've come to it. That longing is always there. Only the intensity toward it changes. Once it gets to a certain point, there's no stopping it. I mean, I guess that's kind of bullshit because I've never really tried to stop it.

I was still working at the video store and living at home two years out of high school. Harriet had roped a poor sucker into marrying her. His name was Sam. He worked down at the grocery store as a general manager. I guess he made decent money. He had a clean apartment, and his car wasn't even two years old. The dude couldn't have weighed more than a hundred and forty pounds, soaking wet. In their wedding photos, they looked like the number 10. My parents watched in their quiet, oblivious way. It was just us now, which was good. Harriet was the only one who'd kept an eye on me. With her out of the way, I could come and go as I pleased without having to make up any bullshit.

The video store gig was paying off. The rental VCRs were being sold as newer models came in, so the viewings kept increasing. It was getting to the point where there was rarely less than a half hour per day without a double feature, and in some cases, I was getting triples. Those were rough. I could easily watch two viewings and hold a conversation in my present reality, but when a third came in, I became nearly comatose. That's what led me back to the old high school. I had outgrown that scene, except for Mrs. Vagle, but I was willing to sacrifice her at that point. The truth was, she'd put on some weight, and her underwear became less desirable.

At the time, I didn't have the same control I have today, which is why I had to sneak in and destroy the TVs to stop the viewings that had given me so much enjoyment. It was the first time I'd done something sneaky that didn't result in someone being killed.

I still had the key to the AV room. Dumbass Spence still never unlocked the front doors until a few minutes before class. A minute after he did, I just walked in and ripped out all the wiring in the back of the TVs. It would have been more satisfying if I'd smashed them, but I didn't want to risk making that much noise. I knew I could have pulled it off. You'd be surprised how getting away with two murders gives you a feeling of complete invincibility. But I thought better of it.

I got mixed results after extinguishing those connections. A week later, my viewings went down by way more than half, but what I didn't expect was the emptiness. I wasn't used to feelings like that. I wasn't used to anything other than the urges. I knew I could feel boredom, longing, and lust, but anything outside of that was new. Knowing what I know now, I realize how unique that is.

It's a lot like when I first saw how to fix that transistor. If you don't talk about it with anyone, how do you know how others' feelings or experiences compare to yours?

I read half of a philosophy book once. I read it while working at the video store in between fetching the cassettes. It was boring as shit, but one part really stuck out to me. It was a simple statement that has always stayed with me. It was more complex than this, but the gist was that the only way you can learn about yourself is through interactions with others. I have never read a truer statement. If I thought nothing about killing someone, how in the hell was I supposed to know it was wrong unless someone else could explain *why* it was wrong? I'm no philosopher, but what I later learned to be sadness—I was missing the connection to the school—is what brought me to my first therapy session, where I began to learn how different I was.

I had enough dough to pay someone but didn't want to go through that bullshit, mainly because I didn't want to fill out a mountain of forms. I found a pretty good solution two towns over in Damatson. Every Friday night, in the basement of a church, they held community forums and offered free counseling. That wasn't completely true. They did ask for donations, but it wasn't mandatory. I made a big deal out of dropping twenty dollars into the box, so the old bitch at the door would think I was a genuine type of guy. The money never made it into the box. I just flashed it and then palmed it before pretending to push it through the slot.

The rooms were full of a collection of losers who thought hanging in groups somehow elevated them to something else. Of all of them, the biggest group was alcoholics. I hated staring at them as they drank that shitty coffee and chain-smoked.

When I ventured in that night, I met Ms. Stacey, the psychologist who gave free sessions. She was plump but pretty, maybe forty. I was sly and asked roundabout questions, disguising the real questions that I wanted to ask, the way they do on the idiot television shows Harriet used to watch. Honestly, I didn't know what was considered acceptable or not. To me, there was nothing wrong with saying I had stabbed some a-hole jock because I didn't want to be kicked out of school. I knew it *should* be wrong, but I just didn't feel it. It was kind of like those arranged marriages you hear about. Someone tells you to love someone because it's in everyone's best interests, so the couple does it, not for love, but just being aware that they should.

So, I made up an elaborate story about missing my friends from high school, even though I wasn't close to them, just to see what she had to say. She gave me some nearly insightful answers, but I was growing impatient. I knew, at best, that I could go there maybe twice. I was paranoid about sharing too much, so then I did something that became a pattern in my life. I took a risk without thinking.

I told her that I was picked on a lot in high school and had fantasies about killing some of the bigger kids who tormented me. Over time, I found that lies that were close to the truth almost always worked. The kids in school had picked on me relentlessly, but honestly, I'd never blamed them. I just figured they'd sensed my weirdness. It was like those documentaries I'd get stuck watching with my dad from time to time on Saturdays after the soldering repair so long ago.

There was an order to things in the natural world. Animals had an instinctive sense that gave them a place and meaning in relation to their surroundings, and when they encountered anything that triggered them, they went on the attack.

As I've thought about it over the years, that's what I believe makes me different. That sense is missing in me. I not only have no barometer pointing me to what is right or wrong, but I also have no desire to develop one.

I had a sort of half-assed theory that everyone's brain would live up to a certain potential based on the geography up there. The area where connection, love, and understanding should be in my brain was filled with the ability to view. It's kind of funny how the thing that makes me unique is also the thing that alienates me from others.

Now, with Ms. Stacey, I was trying to figure out what kind of bra she was wearing. Her sweater was tight but had a weird, quilted pattern, making identifying it difficult. With her wild smile, she told me that it was normal to feel aggressive like this. Finally, progress. Someone was showing me behind the curtain, which always seemed to be closed. I went a little further and told her that I'd even planned how I would do it. She explained that this was also normal and asked about my parents. Then, I opened up more than I'd planned and told her about the nothingness of our relationship.

I told her about the day they locked me in the closet because I was being too loud, and admittedly, I really *was* being obnoxious that day. It was the day after my fourth birthday, and I couldn't get my toy car track to stay together. I also told her how I screamed myself to sleep that night in the dark. I could see she found that distressing.

She had to be wearing one of those Cross Your Heart bras. Harriet had a few like that, as they were the only things that could contain her. Ms. Stacey asked if that was the first time I'd ever spoken to someone about that incident. When I answered yes, she scribbled something down in a notebook. I didn't like that, but I tolerated it, figuring she had no way of knowing who I really was, so nothing she wrote could follow me anywhere.

She went on to explain that children who were abused in such a way often found it hard to get along with others in their same age group. She said that they usually aren't able to feel safe or trust anyone because of their betrayal.

I was getting really bored. If I hadn't been viewing some bald guy laying into his fat-ass wife, I probably would have walked out. They were trying to mimic the porno they were watching, and it was hilarious listening to them repeating back the ridiculous lines that were meant for better-looking people.

Thinking these meetings only lasted an hour at most, I interrupted as she made a passionate speech, trying to get me to open up about anything physical that might have happened to me. I really thought about lifting my shirt and showing her the something physical that had caused the scars across my back, but I finally decided to cut to the chase. That was another one of my grandma-isms that I was really fond of. I flat out asked her how many visions she saw in a day. By how she looked, you would have thought I had asked her if she'd ever been double- penetrated.

I will openly admit that I've never been good with facial expressions. I notice differences in facial muscles. I have very good vision, but I just don't always understand what faces mean when they change. I always have to wait for words to interpret the movement for me.

When she said, "I don't quite understand," I thought perhaps it was a game to get me to open up more. I pretty much knew that not everyone got an instruction book on how to fix things, but I had no idea at all that someone smart, like a doctor didn't see multiple things at once. I caught on quick that I'd botched it up by asking, and now I wanted to leave.

Instead, I ignored the viewing, which wasn't easy because the bald guy had just pulled out a thick belt, and I listened to Ms. Stacey. If I had to guess, I would say her expression was compassionate as she placed the notebook down and leaned forward with her elbows on her thighs. The motion put the Cross Your Heart Bra to the test. She stared right into my eyes—I always hated that—and asked me what I saw. I backtracked and told her I didn't see actual visions. I just saw myself wanting to do things in my mind. She grilled me on that. She was a sharp one, trying to open me up again, but I thought I did a good job of convincing h er.

When our time was up, she gave me her card, wrote her home number on the back, and asked me to promise her that I would come back the following week. I thanked her, and when I did, I meant it. With her home number, it would be easy to track her down now if I decided to kill her.

The next week, I didn't go back. It wasn't from fear or anything like that. I thought Ms. Stacey was either a liar or stupid. She had to know that some, if not all, people saw visions. From my perspective, they had to.

Maybe she acted like she didn't because that subject was one of those subtle things that polite people didn't ask about. Mrs. Vagle had been the first to introduce me to that phrase when she caught me asking my schoolmate Pat if she used a vibrator. Thinking back on it, Ms. Stacey had the same look on her face as Mrs. Vagle had as she sat me down and explained that she wouldn't send me to the principal if I promised I understood what I'd done wrong. I'd done what I always did—I lied.

My next big adventure was trying to find a replacement for the old AV TVs. The VCRs were still paying off, but DVD players were slowly replacing them. The moron who owned Galaxy Video refused to buy any of the new machines, as he told us they were a fad, so he wasn't going to waste time on them. The dude had always been a dipshit.

I had a few additions to my schedule, a TV or a car radio here or there, but I was desperate to get my fix. You'd be amazed at how many people just sat and watched their VCRs and did nothing interesting.

An idea formed when I bought new sheets at BMart, the one and only department store in our town. As the idiot behind the register struggled with three quarters to count out the exact change, I noticed the closed-circuit television screen behind the acne-scarred a-hole in his striped smock. If I could tap into each camera, it would be like striking oil in your backyard as you were digging for a fence post. I left the store, scheming up a way to get in there at night.

As I tried to figure out a way to bypass the security system, I stood beneath the nearest outdoor camera. If I came up tight against the wall, there was no way it could capture my image. But, with a little planning, it could work. As I'd done with Mary Louise's parents' house, I cased the place over the next few days. The best plan was to get to the main terminal. I assumed this was in the manager's office at the back of the store, next to the returns and complaint department. Without asking, I had no way of telling, but it was the most logical location.

On a Tuesday, just after lunch, I once again acted without thinking. Standing in the gift wrap and card aisle for way too long, I watched the blonde woman who managed the store walk into her office. There was no camera in this hallway, and the returns desk was empty. I took this as a sign and acted.

I walked up to the door and grabbed the handle, but it was locked. The plan had been to open the door, see what was inside, and say I thought it was the bathroom. While my hand was still on the knob, someone pulled the door open.

About a foot away from me was the ridiculously hair-sprayed hairdo of the manager. She kind of frowned and giggled at the same time, saying, "You startled me. Can I help you with something?"

For the life of me, I don't know why I reacted the way I did. Maybe it was because she looked like a skinny version of Harriet. Maybe it was because I was really hurting for more viewings. It was the first time I had felt anger before I killed. In the way that I'd practiced so many times in my mirror, I buried the knife in her face so fast that her facial expression didn't have a chance to change. The serrated edge did its job; there wasn't even a scream.

In that moment, I fully appreciated the power the longing had over me. The wave of pleasure that came over me was not remotely close to anything I'd ever experienced. Knowing this wasn't the place to relax, I grabbed the slumping woman by her suit jacket and bra—not sure which kind, but it sure was tight—and pushed her into the room. I locked the door behind me and cleaned my knife. I felt amazingly calm. I learned later that this wasn't unusual, especially if there has been a lot of time between kills, but it was a first back then.

I sat in the office chair behind her desk and felt pretty fucking smart because next to the desk was a wall of screens with a control panel beneath them.

Looking at the screens, I was confident that no one saw what had just happened. I took my knife, flipped open the control panel, and ripped apart the wiring and circuitry of the camera feeds. While I waited for the instruction book, I moved the photo of the manager and her family face down. I remember reading in the paper later that they thought the killer had done this because they felt guilty and because the family was staring at them. Dumb a-holes. I did it because her daughter was an ugly pig, and I couldn't deal with looking at her.

I placed my hand on the keyboard, and the instructions led the way. Looking at what it was going to take to fix it, I wanted to kick myself for making it so complicated, but I knew the effort would be worth it if I could view all the cameras at once. I had every tool imaginable inside the pocket of my new army surplus jacket, and I was glad I did. Half an hour later, I had the circuit board back together again. While I had access to the instructions, I also saw how to erase the twenty-four tapes. So, I erased them and put on a ten-minute delay to cover my tracks.

The whole time, I felt like someone was going to knock on the door, but never once did this bother me. It just helped me stay focused and ready with the knife. When I was done, I wiped the place down. I have no idea if this mattered, but I did it anyway. Then, I propped up the manager in her chair and walked out of the store.

As I made my way down the aisle, scanning for anyone nearby who could have seen me leaving the room, I was viewing a family watching a dumb-ass movie about a professor who had shrunk his family. I felt complete. If everyone around me felt like I did right then, I finally understood what TV and philosophy books couldn't teach me: Life was about experiences.

These moments give you purpose and fulfillment. It reminded me of an advertisement I once saw in a comic that I used to think was lame. The tagline said, "Be high on life!" and the characters were all high-fiving one another. I admit, if I'd had a friend, I would have high-fived them right then. That was until I saw Mark Sullivan.

He was buying a quart of oil and some beef jerky from the jerk at the register. I was so fucking close to getting out of there clean, until that Cro-Magnon a-hole turned his head. He looked right at me without nodding, but I knew he recognized me. Like I said, facial expressions are not easy for me, but I knew I had to kill him.

Mark was a few years older than me. I'd met him at Galaxy Video. He was the one who had trained me how to grab the tags and pull the movies from the back. The dude was a real genius, mastering such a complex skill. We'd only worked together for a short time—the boss had caught him swiping films. The gay kind. The one he'd gotten caught had a cover with two shirtless dudes working on a hot rod. I was the only one in back when he was let go, and the look he gave me then was the same look he was giving me now.

My high didn't completely deflate, but I wasn't too pleased with needing to share it. Knowing what had to be done, I did something that I absolutely hate. I made eye contact with him and smiled as I walked out of the store. It took some practice, but at this point, I was getting pretty good at it. I knew I had little time to make a decision. The camera delay lasted only a few minutes.

I saw his "Stang," which I had always heard him calling his Mustang, so it kind of stuck. The guy was really into cars, and he had this one decked out. It had the engine coming through the hood and other enhancements I didn't give two shits about.

The plan came to me quickly, so I walked up to it and leaned against the driver's side, knowing I needed to take care of this now.

I couldn't chance him seeing a news report and calling in, saying he'd seen me there. Maybe I was being paranoid, but I wasn't going to end this high. Mark left the store and came up to me.

I guess he found me sexually attractive because when I asked him for a ride, he simply said, "Sure, jump in."

We got out of there quickly enough to beat out the camera. Trying to impress me, he peeled out of the parking lot, shooting smoke and gravel into the air and making a shitload of noise. Knowing we were now out of range of the cameras, I felt calm and, I guess, superior, like I was meant to be doing these things because if I wasn't, it wouldn't have been this easy.

On that day of firsts, I let Mark drive me to the local forest preserve, knowing full well that he was trying to seduce me. When we pulled into the wooded area, the parking lot was empty. As soon as we backed into the space, he leaned over and put his hands between my legs without warning. I really don't know why, but I didn't resist. I even let him kiss me. Inside, I felt nothing. It wasn't because he was a man. My sexual tastes revolved around women's clothing.

The people who wore them meant nothing more than adding shape to what I desired.

This being my first sexual experience on my day of firsts, I was willing to let it play out. I really wasn't sure how this worked other than what I'd seen in a few viewings. He already had his pants down, and if he hadn't pulled up my shirt the way he did, I would have let him do whatever he wanted.

Once my shirt was up, he saw the hunting knife in its sheath. His eyes got really wide, giving me a good target, but I missed anyway. He turned at the very last second, and the tip went right into his ear. At that angle, it stopped as it struck bone in his neck.

I'll give it to him. The dude was tough and fast. He screamed and grabbed the knife's handle. I guess that hurt a lot because the second he touched it, the wound started to gush. I knew I could finish him off quickly and easily, but I just sat back and enjoyed the show. With blood shooting at the windshield, he opened the door and tried to run. He didn't make it two steps before his pants caught him up, and he fell flat on his face. I climbed across the car and stood above him. He grasped at the ground, for I don't know what

.

As I knelt to finish him off, he rolled over, smacking my thigh with his boner. The thing was huge. One good jab and the knife finished him off. When I got back to the car, I pulled out the radio faceplate and rewired it. I figured anyone driving a car like that might give me some interesting viewings.

That afternoon, I had a long walk back to my parents' house. It gave me time to think. As I walked along the road, I had two overlapping viewings. Both were boring, just families going about their stupid-ass lives.

It was cold, or else I would have ditched my jacket. It had a lot of blood on it, but it was a checkered camouflage, so it blended in pretty good. Eventually, a squad car passed. My heart didn't skip a beat, even as it slowed down. I just kept walking, focusing on the viewings. The car kept going without lighting up, and I was grateful for that. I knew I could have taken care of the cop, but didn't feel quite up to it. I was coming down slightly from the high in a good way and didn't want anything to change. It was one of those perfect moments, a moment when you feel like you are floating above all the bullshit that life puts you through.

Walking along, I pulled the collar up to my chin. I could smell the manager lady on the coat. Right then, I knew I was in deep. This time, there wouldn't be a two-year gap until the next adventure. Honestly, I doubted I could hold out for much longer than two weeks. It was nearly two hours before I got home. As soon as I got back, I wrapped the jacket in a plastic garbage bag. I would dump it the first chance I got. Until then, it would be safe in my closet. I knew I was clear, but I flipped on the news as I warmed up my turkey TV dinner.

The next few years brought a lot of change. Harriet had her first baby. The kid took after her; it was probably one of the fattest babies ever born. She brought the porker to our parent's house every Sunday night for dinner. Even though it made her suspicious, I rarely went upstairs to visit. I didn't like the change in my routine. On Sunday nights, I'd managed two excellent back-to-back viewings. Both were women's groups, and they wore the most amazing clothes, trying to look respectful as they looked for support.

Because it was a weekend, I would allow myself a more expensive chicken-fried steak instead of my usual turkey while watching. I'd found that, by viewing BMart's surveillance, multiple cameras were the way to go. It was rare when one of the cameras didn't pick up at least one really good viewing. By then, my VCRs weren't really paying out anymore, as DVDs had taken over, proving the dumbass video store owner wrong and almost closing up Galaxy Video. I didn't work there anymore, as there had been several complaints about me—a-holes talking about me not moving fast enough. I would like to see how fast any of them moved if they saw three things at once, like I did. Surprisingly, I was still living off the dentist's money and the couple of bucks I had taken off folks when I was on my adventures. I didn't have many bills other than my TV dinners, so I didn't sweat it.

When I took over the basement, my dad demanded rent. We had a conversation, and I straightened him the fuck out. The few times he saw me in the house after that, he backed away quick. It's kind of sad watching someone who you used to look up to acting like a pussy, but hey, I got my way.

I visited another shrink. That guy wasn't quite the same as Ms. Stacey. Halfway through, he got pretty aggressive, and that was the first time I had ever heard the word *sociopath*.

Unfortunately for him, I opened up a little too much. It was his last session, but it certainly wasn't mine. I'd gone there because the killings were getting out of control. It was rare when I didn't kill at least one person every month—sometimes more. At that pace, I had to figure out how to curb the urges because I knew deep down that stopping them for any prolonged period was no longer an option.

I was smart about how I did them. Unless it was a special circumstance, I didn't kill in my own town anymore. It was amazingly easy to get away with the killings when you had no association with the victim. I killed most of them in the same "Mary Louise" way, knife to the eye. Looking back, it was dumb to do them like that. It left a traceable pattern and made them less random. I learned this by watching the interviews on the news. Even though I knew I should change this, I couldn't. There was no point in killing if I wasn't doing it this exact way. I guess I was no better than an addict chasing their high.

As I was evolving, I read all I could about psychology. I wasn't exactly confused by the books, but I still didn't understand them. There was way too much about feelings for me to even grasp what I was reading. If I could just get a few answers, I could kill in a fashion that was less risky.

Killing on the road was getting expensive. I managed that by taking out a few guys who didn't fit the standard profile that the news kept talking about. I would look for expensive cars in motel parking lots, using my dad's Olds whenever I left town. We had an understanding now. I didn't even ask; I just took it. Almost every time, I would find the owner of the car in bed with a prostitute. The good thing about that was that there was always cash.

The doors in those places might as well have been made out of cardboard, so one good kick and I was in, taking the old fucker out and then the whore. Killing them was business. There was too much noise to do the things I wanted to do, but they paid very well. That is until I learned what a pimp was.

I was twenty-four at the time, cruising through a dump called the Walacondo Motel, when I saw an S-Class. Knowing it would pay off, I did what I always did, parked the Olds across the street, and walked. By then, I'd dumped the Army jacket. There had been multiple reports of a possible suspect wearing an army jacket near the scene, so now I alternated hooded sweatshirts. The place was more than a dump; it was barely standing. I easily went through the door. It wasn't even locked.

The old dude somehow reminded me of Mark Sullivan. He jumped out of the bed with his pants around his ankles, his boner bouncing around. A quick jab with the hunting knife shut him the fuck up quick.

The prostitute must have been a gymnast. She tumbled backward off the bed. That was something to see, because she was almost completely naked. Although athletic, she wasn't too bright. She mistimed her spin and cracked her head on the nightstand, the only thing in the room that looked sturdy. It was pretty funny to watch. The look of surprise on her face when she struck it was fucking priceless.

That was, until I heard a grunt, and a bat slammed into my shoulder. Sparks flared through my vision. I'd caught some beatings in my day, but never anything like that. Maybe it was the shock, but most likely, it was the size of the dude who'd swung. I went down hard, but had enough brains to roll when I hit the ground. If I hadn't done that just then and in that exact way, I would have been dead.

On my back, I could see what had to be a four-hundred-pound dude wearing an Adidas tracksuit swinging the bat with both hands, bringing it down right where my head had been before I rolled. He used so much force that the bat cracked in half as it hit the shitty-ass carpeted floor. This put him slightly off balance.

I tried to use this to my advantage and stab him with my left arm, but it was a no-go. Whatever had happened when the bat made contact with my shoulder, it fucked up that arm.

When the big dude saw the knife, he took a half-step back, and his foot stepped directly on the arm of the old man, causing him to fly back onto the bed. I knew that was my best chance of getting out of there in one piece, but I didn't run. The door was right there, open and right in front of me, but I slowly sat up, ignoring the pain. The truth was, I wanted that money.

I had other thoughts. I guess they were my version of what the shrinks would call a fight- or-flight response, but those were really quiet. They usually got that way when things were moving fast. I guess that was the one big advantage of having thoughts without any emotions. It made me more instinctual. I didn't react to a feeling because, the fact was, I didn't really have any. Somewhere deep in my head, I just thought, *Hey, if you leave now, you can outrun this fat a-hole*. Instead, I chose to listen to the other thought. It told me that I wanted that old dude with the funny boner's money, because that money would stop me from needing a job for my TV dinners. The whole thing was simple, and I like simple.

All these ideas took about two seconds. I am really good at listening, and right then, I heard nothing outside the room that would change my mind. The only noise was the fat ass wheezing as he tried to roll out of the bed. Always agile, even with the injury, I kind of karate- flipped myself to my feet. Unfortunately, I had no room for style. If that guy got hold of me, he would have wrestled me to death, so I plunged the knife into his sternum. He bled like a geyser and whined like a child as he gripped the wound with his disgusting sausage fingers.

With him docile, I made a quick cut to his throat to stop the noise. Knowing he was done, I poked my head outside the door and confirmed that I could still trust what I always thought was superhuman hearing. There was no movement outside.

Now, I'm not a total idiot. I knew someone behind one of the curtained windows could be calling the cavalry, but in a neighborhood like that, a responder would take at least ten minutes if they showed up at all.

I felt good enough to close the door and search the place. The fat ass was almost gone. I decided to wait to search him until I knew he was. Looking through, I saw that the old dude's pants didn't have a wallet or cash in them. My first thought was that the whore had already swiped it. She was lying in a huddled mess with her neck against the leg of the nightstand.

All she had on was a bra and a frayed jean skirt. It looked like cut-offs with actual pockets. I carefully made my way around the big dude—I wasn't up for one of those horror- movie final jump scares—and grabbed her by the shoulder. As soon as I made contact with her, I saw instructions just like I usually did with radios and TVs. The only difference was that this wasn't showing me how to rewire a piece of plastic. I was seeing how to perform a tracheotomy. I'm not going to lie. I didn't know that word at the time. I looked it up later.

I viewed how to bend her head back and cut into her airway. I wasn't generally in the business of helping the dying, but having never experienced this before, I did what the instructions showed me.

Once the knife pierced the larynx—yeah, I didn't know that word either—she gasped for air through her throat. If you have never seen this before, I'm warning you: it's not pretty. Air bubbles push the blood out, and there is a wicked, gurgling noise.

I had to make a choice right then. If she opened her eyes, would I kill her? Fortunately, she didn't. The bruise on her head was nasty, and she just lay there wheezing through her throat hole. I ripped her skirt off and jammed in the back pocket was the old man's wallet. There was nearly a thousand in cash. I was pretty happy that I'd stuck it out. Whenever I'd done this before, the most I'd gotten was four hundred. I put her down with a pillow behind her neck and moved her head to an angle so the blood would flow, as the instructions had shown me. With her head to the side, I immediately understood.

She had some kind of space-age hearing aid jammed into her, with a wire attached behind the earlobe. That had to be why I'd seen how to fix her. Right then, I didn't really think through the significance of being linked to a human. Honestly, all I thought was, how many people did she have to blow to get that in her ear, and was it worth it?

It was still quiet, but I didn't want to push it too far, I was eager to get moving. So I got into the fat man's pocket. The material of his pants was super thin. As I dug around, I felt all the flab of his midsection. It was worth it. He had nearly four thousand in small bills.

My internal clock was ticking, so I pulled back the curtain and peeked through the glass. There was no movement. I walked out the door, put my hood up, and headed to my dad's Olds, covered in three different types of blood.

By then, I had enough experience to have the trunk rigged. I shed the sweatshirt and wrapped it in a plastic bag. On my way back home, I was starving. I was going to try a drive-thru but toughed it out. Knowing I was less than two hours from home, I wanted to celebrate the addition to my fortune over my favorite dinner.

———

Before I was even a mile away, I had an unscheduled viewing. This one came with a headache like you wouldn't believe, and my throat felt so dry it was like I'd swallowed sandpaper.

Fighting the pain, I pulled over to the side of the road. The viewing was coming from the room I'd just left. It took me a minute to figure it out, but I was seeing what the prostitute was seeing. The view was partially of the bed and the ceiling. There was a well-built woman in a nightie off in the corner, screaming into the phone that she needed an ambulance and rambling off the address. A minute later, she was on her knees, holding our hand—I know "our" is an odd choice of words, but I'm telling you, I felt her hand as if she were sitting beside me in the piece- of-shit car my father spent so much time washing every Saturday morning.

She whispered that everything was going to be all right. As I looked at her for the first time in my life, I could read her face. She honestly cared. I was getting a real good view of her bra. It was one of those push-up ones, with the clasp in front. With all the makeup she had on, I had to guess she worked for fat Adidas on the bed behind her. If she was a whore, I was really surprised that she was sitting there and wasn't out the door.

I guess the gymnast blacked out because the viewing stopped right there. When the connection went black, my head and throat felt instantly better. My hand, though, was curved as if somebody had been holding it.

I sat there in a daze. Beyond the physical pain, I also felt emotional pain. For the first time ever, I felt what I later learned to be sadness and fear. I've got to say, I didn't like it one bit.

I heard sirens off in the distance, so I got back on the interstate and headed back to the basement. Along the way, the new viewing came in a few times. The first flash showed me the paramedics with some type of balloon and a stethoscope. That only lasted a minute. Then, when the next flash came, there were lights rolling over my head down a long-ass hallway.

The second one was rough because I already had two viewings going. One was a dog watching some really handsome guy sleeping on a couch while a dumbass movie about a duck superhero played.

The other was back at BMart. A couple of women were trying on jackets. With only one arm steering and her wounds and emotions coursing through me, I was pretty amazed that I kept the car on the road.

When I got back, my dad sat at the kitchen table, trying to play the tough guy. I stared him down and went downstairs to my room.

I was waiting for the TV dinner to finish in the microwave. It took me some time, but I'd finally figured out to ignore the instructions and cook for exactly seven minutes, which was the only way to make sure the center of the cranberry sauce wasn't frozen.

I flipped on the news. This was the tenth time one of my adventures had been on TV. The news lady wore a white turtleneck with a lacy bra beneath. You had to really look to see it, but it was there.

The story she spouted off was that a solicitation appeared to have gone horribly wrong.

She didn't give any graphic details or names; she only said that the police had received the information from an anonymous call. I knew Nightie was a prostitute, so she must have flown out of there right after the gymnast had passed out. However, I did wonder how much time she'd spent looking through her old boss's sweatpants and searching for all her hard-earned cash. They went back to the studio and babbled on about the election. I flipped it off and ate a second dinner. I didn't always splurge like that, but it had been a big night.

Around four in the morning, the viewing came back. The headache was gone, but my throat hurt like a motherfucker, and my shoulder ached.

This time, the viewing was a doctor arguing with two guys who had to be plainclothes detectives. They won the argument and started the barrage of questions. Even though the gymnast couldn't talk, I could see what she was writing. The two a-holes questioning her were relentless. She played dumb. It couldn't be too hard for her, but I could feel when she was lying as she used the magic marker to write out the simple yes-or-no answers. The only one that really mattered to me was when they asked her if she could describe the man who'd done this. It was a simple no. That was good because I felt frustration, so I knew she was telling the truth. Let me tell you, having emotions come at you like that all at once without an instruction book is rough. I had no idea what was going on or how to deal with them. All I knew was that if they kept going on like that, I had to kill her.

Then I had a real out-there thought. If I could feel her pain, would I also be able to feel what she felt when she died? I didn't feel anything when I thought this, but I knew this had changed me somehow. For the first time, I pondered the future, and the consequences associated with those thoughts. It might be impossible for someone who wasn't like me to believe this, but this was not how my brain worked. Typically, there were things that I needed and wanted, and I did what was necessary to get them. Now, it was different. I didn't learn *how* different until later.

I couldn't figure out why, but this viewing wasn't following the rules. Instead of just an hour a week, now it was always present, except for when she slept. There was also a connection to her feelings, both emotional and physical. Whenever she was awake, my throat ached, and I could feel fear and loneliness. I knew I needed to figure this out, but I also knew it wouldn't be easy.

I couldn't do much. My shoulder wasn't wrecked, but I had to pay real close attention to it. My left arm was a struggle. I wasn't going to use up my TV dinner money on an a-hole doctor, so I dealt with it. During those first few days, I never left my room. It was all right. I had enough food for a couple of weeks, and I had my regular viewings to keep me busy. It would have been great if I hadn't had that woman there all the time.

Her name was Penelope, but she went by Penny. I learned that she lived with two other girls. Neither was much to look at, and neither knew she was a hooker. Some of this I knew from the conversations they had or, should I say, from *them* talking to *her*. She still couldn't talk, which meant I couldn't talk, which was total shit. How is that fair?

I knew some of what was going on with her just because I knew, the same way that I knew I would be calm when putting a knife into someone. I knew things about this Penny. Most times, I could see parts of her past, but more than that, I could feel her.

I could feel her shame when the other girls looked at her. The shame because they accepted her as one of them, one of the privileged who got to stay in the apartment off-campus, except she didn't have a rich daddy to pay her part. My Penny had to suck off disgusting old men to pay her way. I could feel her at odds with fooling them into thinking she was just like them. It was very disorienting, but I could feel the anxiety she felt about them somehow finding out and all the paranoid thoughts that the cops would show up at the door and expose her and the fake life she'd created. They would reveal her real life, where her mother was dead, and her father used up the monthly disability check to drink himself into oblivion every night, leaving her to make it on her own.

I could feel how hard she worked in school, surviving on the hot lunch they gave her because there wasn't any food at home. How she knew if she could graduate from college, she could get a job and have the life she'd dreamed of as a little girl. I could feel the day the acceptance letter had come, then the last line talking about budget cuts and how her scholarship would cover only half the expenses. I could feel the memory of the pain of her first time in the backseat of an old man's car and how degrading it had been to take the bills from him as he sat there with his boner sticking out of his pants. It was so real that I could feel the pain between my legs and remember telling myself that it would all be worth it once school was done. Then, I could get a real job and wipe all this from my memory. I could feel all this the same way I felt the pain in my shoulder. It didn't take long for me to know that I had to kill her as soon as I was able. Until then, I had no choice but to put up with all those bullshit feelings.

I probably should have just gone to a doctor when the days became weeks. But I started to realize that maybe Penny was special. I just couldn't believe that everyone else could feel like this. With all that inside you, how could you function?

My shoulder wasn't perfect. It had this weird clicking noise, but I felt strong enough to get back out there. Maybe I was pushing too hard, but I had to take care of her. I just couldn't deal with those feelings. This adventure was going to be a chore, and it wasn't going to feel as good. It was too easy being able to see myself coming, but I looked at it like killing old dudes for their cash. It was a means to an end, like my grandma used to say.

Friday was my normal killing night, as usual, always trying to relive Mary Louise, and this Friday looked like Penny was going to be alone. The two homely chicks who lived with her weren't great face wise, but I'd seen the taller one in her bra, which was one of the best viewings I'd ever seen.

When the two chicks begged Penny to go to a concert, my girl refused. I'd still done my homework and checked out the place four nights in a row to see what the neighborhood was like. They lived on the middle floor of an old brownstone. The top and bottom floors had students as well. There was a back stairway without a gate, then narrow alleys separating almost identical buildings flanking her place. There was a shit-ton of windows, so there was a lot of exposure.

This was obviously not ideal, but I knew I would press ahead.

While sharing her thoughts, I knew that she wouldn't venture out alone anytime soon.

She had enough dick-sucking money to last her for a while, and the school had told her to take as much time as she needed to recover. I might have waited even another week, but her period had just started, and I felt her cramps—let me tell you, that is rough, and that pushed me over the edge.

The night came. There was only a partial moon, and there were no streetlights in the back of the buildings. I wore my black hooded sweatshirt with a camo tee underneath. After much consideration, I chose the building four houses down as an entry point. It extended the walk, but there were enough shrubs to give me cover. I got to the back of the building and had her constant viewing at the same time as the remaining VCRs, which was good. Although the VCR had a shapely woman, I could tune her out. There were a few lights on, which was preferable because I could see if someone was looking out. It was now or never, so I walked head down, reading along with Penny from what I thought was a trigonometry book.

My throat felt better, but the cold air didn't help much. I made it to the second-floor landing. This wasn't like the bullshit motel doors—it was solid. This was why I always did my homework first. Luck was on my side. Earlier, when Penny had been warming up soup, I'd seen that only one of the deadbolts was locked. I could have made it through two, but it would have put more strain on my shoulder. I pulled the angled crowbar from my pants, and with a good push that made my shoulder click, I got the door open. It was way quieter than I would have thought. She never looked up from her figures. As soon as I was in, I listened for a full minute. It sounded clear.

Knowing the layout, I went down the hall. I'd been down it with Penny so many times that I knew to step around the middle of the floorboard beneath the "Hang in there!" cat poster to avoid the squeak in the hardwood. Feeling intense cramps, I made it into her room, and as she sat there, I viewed what she saw and the back of her head at the same time. Even knowing it was a risk, I had to do it. I had to view her seeing me as the knife came. Knowing it would give her a chance to react, I got within a foot and said with a still-squeaky voice, "Hello, Penny."

I felt her panic as she spun around and then her terror as she saw the knife while viewing myself the whole time. It reminded me of the double vision I used to get when my old man would crack me in the back of the head with the shovel handle, except the images weren't duplicates. I could feel her resignation as she accepted her fate. Quickly, her fear and anger disappeared. There was just emptiness as she finally let go of the dream of her better-after-college life that she'd worked so hard to get.

When the knife went into her eye, I instantly knew what a mistake I'd made. As it struck the skull, I lost sight in my eye and dropped to my knees in pain. Maybe I just had to wait until her heart stopped. Then, I would be all right. A minute went by—no change. Then, a few more. In agony, I felt for her pulse. I knew I didn't have to. She was gone, yet I felt for her pulse anyway. There was nothing there.

Father, that was over a month ago. That's why I'm here *now*. I never believed in the Church, and I'll be honest—at this point, why not — I probably still don't, but I can't think of anyone else to ask.

How much longer is it until a dead person is truly gone?

You see, I never would have believed it, the same way most wouldn't believe in my viewings, but after death, there is conscio usness... and pain. Every day, I can still feel her lying in the darkness of her casket, wishing she could leave.

MORE CHILLS FROM VELOX BOOKS

www.ingramcontent.com/pod-product-compliance
Lightning Source LLC
Chambersburg PA
CBHW020656010826
48969CB00013B/2161